Critics and authors praise
WHAT THE DEAF-MUTE HEARD
by G. D. Gearino

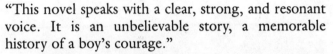

"This novel speaks with a clear, strong, and resonant voice. It is an unbelievable story, a memorable history of a boy's courage."
— Kaye Gibbons, best-selling author of *Sights Unseen*

"Gearino is a talented yarn-spinner, who knows how to concoct a high-velocity story."
— *The Plain Dealer* (Cleveland)

"From Voltaire to Vonnegut, comic authors have created naive characters through whom they cast satirical light upon the foibles of whatever folk they want to make fun of. Voltaire did it in France; Vonnegut did it in Indiana. Now newspaperman and author G. D. Gearino has done it in Georgia. . . ."
— *Winston-Salem Journal* (NC)

"Gearino unleashes a powerful imagination and gift for storytelling. He takes a premise that at face value seems totally implausible and proceeds to craft an intricate tale of intrigue interlaced with homespun observations about the human condition. . . . WHAT THE DEAF-MUTE HEARD is a spellbinding work of fiction."
— *Milwaukee Journal–Sentinel*

Also by G. D. Gearino

Counting Coup

What the Deaf-Mute Heard

G. D. Gearino

This book belongs to -
Brenda Brownridge
April / 99
Costa Rica

POCKET BOOKS
New York   London   Toronto   Sydney   Tokyo   Singapore

This book is a work of fiction. Names, characters, places, and incidents are products of the author's imagination or are used fictitiously. Any resemblance to actual events or locales or persons living or dead is entirely coincidental.

POCKET BOOKS, a division of Simon & Schuster Inc.
1230 Avenue of the Americas, New York, NY 10020

Copyright © 1996 by G. D. Gearino
Cover art copyright © Hallmark Hall of Fame

ISBN 0-671-02073-0

First Pocket Books trade paperback printing December 1997

10 9 8 7 6 5 4 3 2 1

POCKET and colophon are registered trademarks of
Simon & Schuster Inc.

Printed in the U.S.A.

For Karolyn, Meghan, and Evan—my loves.

Acknowledgments

We're required to be humble and sincerely thankful only a few times in life. The writing of this essay is one of those moments.

Many people helped me in specific and significant ways. I've thanked each of them individually and promised to put in a good word on their behalf at Saint Peter's gate. But the efforts of two of them were so overarching as to require a public thanks.

Jane Dystel, my literary agent, along with her staff did a remarkable job of leading me through this realm. Jane is the rarest of beings: things happened exactly when, and as, she said they would happen. She took an armload of loose paper and convinced others it was a book, and for that I am profoundly grateful.

Bob Mecoy at Simon & Schuster likewise has earned a permanent place in my nightly devotions. His editing of the manuscript was flawless. And if this book enjoys commercial success, it's because he was its champion at critical moments. He, too, has my thanks.

I also am grateful to my wife, Karolyn. She rescued me from computer hell countless times and kept everything running while I spent hours in that motionless, near-comatose state that writers call work. (OK, dear, how's that? Now can we put on those little costumes and play that "me Tarzan, you Jane" game?)

Finally, thanks to George and Grace for planting the seed.

1 I've never had a reputation as a story-
teller, which is understandable when you consider I haven't uttered a word since that morning fifty-two years ago when I
stepped off the bus in Barrington. I was a boy of ten, and my
mother had disappeared sometime the night before. I never
saw or heard from her again. I never left Barrington, and in
fact, I never strayed very far from the bus station. I slept in a
room in the back there almost all my life.

I don't talk because I choose not to. As far as everyone in
Barrington is concerned, I'm a deaf-mute. That's not so. In reality, I've heard everything worth hearing in this town. I've
worked in almost every home and office: sweeping, cleaning,
raking, mowing, and fixing. People are remarkably candid with
one another when I'm around. I know who's been sleeping
with whom, who cheats on his taxes, who's in the bad mar-
riages, and who's been to Atlanta for an abortion. Mention
anyone in town and I can tell you whether they're rich or poor,
happy or miserable, frigid or randy, smart or stupid, likely to
succeed or doomed to fail. I know everything that's happened

9

in this town for decades, but most of it's not worth telling. It's the sort of stuff that happens everywhere.

But I will tell you what happened in Barrington during one week in August 1966, when a young preacher-in-training named Perry Ray Pruitt managed to make this Georgia city the focus of a worldwide argument over who was more important, Jesus or John Lennon. He also made the cover of *Life* magazine, helped send a man to jail, and had a municipal parking lot named after him. But all that aside, Perry Ray failed in the one task he set out to accomplish that week: he didn't save a single soul. In a perverse sort of way, he may have even helped me to lose mine.

Before I get on with the story, however, I should explain a few things. I won't pretend that everything I'm about to tell you happened precisely as I set it out here. I'm recalling from memory conversations and incidents that happened a long time ago. And at a few points—when I wasn't around to hear what happened—I've simply made educated calculations of what people said or did. But this story is as true as I can make it.

Think of this as a Homeric tale in reverse. This hasn't been passed orally through the generations, only committed to print so late that the principal characters are long past disputing the details. The written version will exist first, and if anyone mentioned here doesn't like it, I invite them to consult their local ambulance chaser. What can they do? Sue me for pretending to be deaf? I kept my mouth shut, listened when people talked, dawdled over a few desks and poked into a few drawers. In the business world, those skills get you a corner office and regular lunches with the boss where you can slice up your colleagues. The fact that all it got me was a cot in a bus station storeroom and the thin end of a broom was my choice, and I'll live with it.

There's one other thing. I'm not going to riddle this story

with Southern accents and idioms. Barrington may be a Southern city, and some of the things that happened could only take place in the Deep South. But everything else—the greed, the duplicity, the plotting and the lust—is common to all towns, so I'll leave you no chance to wag your head over those strange Southern folk. Setting aside the international uproar that resulted from Perry Ray picking up the newspaper that August morning and having the miracle revealed to him, this is a simple tale that could have happened anywhere.

Barrington is what people often have in mind when they think of Southern cities.

It's set in the low hills northeast of Atlanta, a pretty place with church spires poking up from hardwoods and an old courthouse set in the middle of a wide lawn. It has a few streets with large Greek Revival mansions that house the ruling class; more streets with the modest, well-tended homes of the middle class; a few clumps of trailers and shotgun shacks around the edges of town, where the poor white folks live; and a black community called Buttermilk Bottom. There's a chicken-processing plant, a factory that produces house paint, another factory that manufactures zippers, and—praise be to God, for running a seam of granite so close by—a quarry that produces gravestones for a three-state area.

A dozen or so elementary schools funnel students into two high schools, which in turn send their wards out into the world to help murder chickens or chop rocks. There are thirty-one churches, three farm implement dealers, forty or so police officers, three library branches, zero liquor stores or taverns, and one statue of a Confederate soldier, memorializing the troop of warriors Barrington sent to fight for the cause, most of whom died on their first night away after one of them got drunk and kicked over a lantern in the barn where they were bivouacked.

Or at least that's how Barrington was in 1966, when the world's attention focused on it. A few things have changed—you can now buy alcohol that wasn't made in the woods, for instance—but otherwise, twenty-five years have left hardly a mark.

Like anyone else, I tend to see myself as the point around which all other things pivot, so the center of the universe is the Barrington bus depot, two blocks east of the courthouse. It's an unprepossessing place, as far as centers of the universe go, with several benches in the main waiting area, a ticket counter, a lunch counter, a station manager's office, his-and-her bathrooms, bays for three buses, and a storeroom that I call home. Every morning I clean the bathrooms and sweep the waiting area. In the evening I pick up trash from the parking lot and bus bays. Once a week, I clean the windows and mop the place. Several times a day, I also check my box behind the ticket counter to see what other work has come in. A system has developed over the years. When people need work done around their homes, they call the station manager and describe the job and how much it pays. The manager makes a note and drops it in my box. On days when perhaps only one or two jobs are called in, I do them for whatever pay is offered. But if I have a number to choose from, I'll take the best job and let the others sit in the box. I know from experience which jobs have a glass of tea and a sandwich included, for instance, and I know that if I ignore certain unpleasant jobs for a day or two—like cleaning gutters on a home with a steep roof—a second request eventually will come in, but with more money offered. Everyone in town knows my system.

There have been only three station managers since I arrived fifty-two years ago. Jenkins, the first, was the one who volunteered to let me stay in the storeroom that first night. He'd set up a cot there for naps and didn't know quite what else to do with me after the policeman had left. I liked old Jenkins. He was a kindly soul who'd been punished by life early and harshly: his wife and daughter had died the same day in a terrible influenza epidemic in 1918. Jenkins ran the bus terminal for nearly forty years, until the morning he was found dead in his car out back.

I despised McAdoo, the second station manager. He never once referred to me by name; I was "the dummy." He had a loud cracker voice and enforced the white-only rule in the waiting room and bathrooms with the true vigor of a lifelong bigot. Where Jenkins, when the terminal was empty, would go outside to ask an old mammy if she needed to use the bathroom, McAdoo painted a line on the ground around a bench and hung a sign that said "Negro Waiting Area," first making sure it was a spot that got no shade. He eventually was fired, after the bus company got a string of letters complaining about him. They were good letters, too, although I was certain I'd gotten permanent writer's cramp before the company finally responded.

The current station manager is Burdeen, who worries that his time in Barrington is a kink in his straight-line ascent to his dream job: district scheduling manager. He swears it's all he's ever wanted. I wonder what his parents thought when they asked the young Burdeen what he wanted to be when he grew up—a cowboy or a baseball player, perhaps—and he answered, "I hope someday to be in charge of maintaining bus schedules, with an eye toward maybe creating an early-morning weekday express run to Atlanta."

Having never had any ambition myself, I'm mystified by it in others. I've watched events in Barrington for five decades from the safety of my silence, and it seems to me that striving isn't nearly as important as just surviving long enough to find out what you're good at. The happiest people I know are the ones who discovered a knack for something—growing roses, handling a wedge in a sand trap, or writing haiku.

Then again, seventeen syllables of poetry may fit better on a gravestone, but they're not nearly as useful as a district bus schedule.

2

Call me Sammy. I arrived at the Barrington bus depot early one spring morning in 1940, sound asleep in the window seat of a cruiser that had reached the end of its run. On the first day of my life as a deaf-mute, I was awakened by the driver, different from the one driving the night before, who shook my shoulder and said, "Wake up, son. Everybody's got to get off now. Is someone meeting you?"

The answer was no. When I'd fallen asleep the previous night, my mother was sitting next to me. When the driver shook me awake, she was gone. Aside from the suitcase she'd tucked into the overhead bin, there was no trace of her.

Life until then hadn't been generous, but at least it had been predictable. My mother and I had shared a run-down apartment in an area of Birmingham, Alabama, populated by mill workers, mechanics, and other inhabitants of the lower reaches of the social strata whose common bond was that they weren't black. It was a ragged, rough neighborhood, with lawns that were trimmed only perhaps twice a summer and decorated with vehicles in various stages of disassembly. There was

a mill nearby where many of the local men worked, an imposing brick structure with transom windows all around, from
which the deafening noise of cotton being processed into cloth
spilled into the neighborhood. The mill often would shut its
operations without notice for weeks at a time, leaving my
neighbors to grow visibly more gaunt as they sat on stoops and
porches, endlessly debating the wisdom of returning to the
hardscrabble farms from which they'd fled to find work in the
city.

Being now well on the far side of sixty years old, I find
that I have fewer and fewer clear memories of that time. I know
I went to school; I can even remember the names of a couple of
teachers and a handful of schoolmates. And I can remember
the home I shared with my mother, a second-story, two-room
apartment that you entered through the kitchen. It was typical
of the housing available in those times, I suppose: a single tap
in the kitchen provided water, a single toilet on each floor
hosted all buttocks, and baths were taken in a large galvanized
tub placed on the floor and filled by hand. The yard was given
over to crops, with each apartment's matron carefully tending
a few cornstalks and beanpoles.

All except my mother, that is. Something I remember well
is that she was different from the other adults in the neighborhood. She didn't work, for one thing, but we never seemed to
need money until the days just before I awoke alone on the
bus. And she was pretty, for another thing. Unlike the mothers
of my playmates, who all shared a pinched and underprivileged
look, my mother still had some juice in her. Men paid attention to her, and she enjoyed that. She had dates, which she
called "engagements," but I never met any of her suitors, nor
do I know how she met them. She would leave me alone with
my dinner and invariably return late, long after I'd fallen asleep
in some random spot in the apartment. But she always re-

turned. If she'd wanted to abandon me, she'd had numerous opportunities to do so before vanishing from the bus that night. It took me years to come around to that point, then another few years before I figured out what happened.

I can recall only two conversations between us. The first occurred when I was perhaps six, and was being taunted by my playmates about my peculiar circumstance.

"Why don't I have a daddy?" I asked one night. It was a rare evening when she was home, and I can remember her standing before the stove preparing a meal.

"You do have a daddy. Everybody's got a daddy," she said.

"Who is he?"

"He's a very important man who lives in another town," she said.

"Why doesn't he come see us?" I asked.

"He's not allowed to," she said. "He has another family, and daddies are supposed to have only one family. So he has to stay with his other family."

I pondered this a moment, then asked: "What's his name?"

"He asked me not to tell anybody, but when you're older, I'll tell you. But you have to keep it a secret."

"Why?"

"Because if his other family finds out about us, they'll be very angry at him. And then he'll be angry at us."

"What's he like?"

"Lots of people are afraid of him, but he's really a gentleman," she said. "I used to work for him, you know."

"You did?"

"I worked in his office. But before you were born, he wanted us to move, so that's why we live here."

The other conversation I recall happened a few years later and it, too, was about my father. We had become poverty-

17

stricken literally overnight. The check my mother was accustomed to receiving in the mail each month didn't come, which sent her off in search of a public telephone. She returned with a haunted look.

"Your daddy's dead," she said. "We don't have any money."

"How do you know he's dead?" I asked.

"Because I just called his office and the woman who answered said he was dead. Said he was buried two weeks ago. She asked what I was calling about and when I said it was about a check, she asked if I wanted to make a claim against the estate."

"What's that mean?" I said.

She looked grim and was quiet for a moment. Finally she said, "It means I'd better check the bus schedules."

The next day she packed our clothes into a single bag, and rummaged around in a drawer until she found a large envelope. "We'll need this," she said. She then wrote a note to the neighbors explaining we'd be back in a week or so, tacked it to the apartment door, and we set off on foot for the bus station.

We left Birmingham late that afternoon. We didn't have enough money for two tickets, but my mother was not without her charm. It was an overnight trip on a mostly empty bus, so the man at the ticket window put us both on with one fare. As we settled into a pair of seats halfway down the aisle, my mother gave me a hug, holding my head hard against the red silk blouse she was wearing, a special one she normally reserved for her engagements.

"We'll have to be sure to get some sleep on this old bus tonight," she said. "We won't be there until morning, and we'll want to look fresh."

She didn't tell me where we were going. As the bus droned through the darkening Alabama countryside, I stared out the window, fascinated by this world beyond my neighborhood. The land was mostly empty, interrupted only by the occasional farm or town where we stopped to pick up a passenger or let one off. By the time night was thoroughly upon us, the air had grown cool and my mother leaned over me to shut the window. I was drowsy, made tired by the excitement, and I pulled my legs up under me and leaned my head into the corner formed by the edge of the bus seat and the windowpost. I felt her kiss my forehead.

"Good night, little one," she said. "Everything will be different tomorrow."

3 It's hard to describe the emptiness and panic I felt as I got off the bus the next morning. I remembered going to sleep with my mother sitting beside me, her face highlighted by the glow from the dashboard. Twice I had stirred awake briefly: once when it must have started raining, as I remembered hearing the sound of the windshield wipers; the other when the bus stopped for a while and I was disturbed by the stillness after its rattling had lulled me to sleep. But otherwise I slept as only a child could, curled into a ball with my face snug against the scratchy seat fabric.

When the driver shook me awake the next morning, it was as if I'd been dropped into another world. The bus was empty, the few other passengers having already collected their bags and made their way somewhere else. Sunlight streamed in through the window, warming my face, but the seat where she'd been was cool, giving no hope that she'd only just gotten up. I was slumped down and I suppose the driver never saw me until he took a last stroll down the aisle to check for forgotten luggage.

"Wake up, son."

There was no sign of her, no smell of her, nothing left behind. I sat there dumbly, unsure what to do.

"C'mon, young fella, you have to get off," the driver said, impatience creeping into his voice. "This bus ain't going anywhere else. This is the end of the line."

I still didn't move, so the driver took me by the arm and led me off. The sun was bright and warm in the deserted parking lot. He returned to the bus, then stepped off again a moment later carrying a bag I recognized as my mother's, which he sat against the station wall, beneath the roof's overhang, next to several other boxes that appeared to be freight. I could see a few people stirring inside the station, but otherwise it was still. I stood in the middle of the lot, with a tightness in my chest that made it hard to breathe. I could hear the driver behind me, as he returned to the bus again to remove his belongings.

"Go sit on the bench over there and wait," he said. Again, I didn't move, and again he took me by the arm and led me to a long wooden bench that served as an outdoor waiting area. "You act like you can't hear a thing. Just sit here. Someone will be along for you directly."

I suppose I should, in the interest of drama and narrative drive, describe how something in my heart told me I'd never see my mother again, how a cloud passed before the sun at that tragic moment, darkening my future forever. This is the point where I should tell how loving and nurturing my mother had been, and how this dark Dickensian twist destroyed my happy little world. I could write that, and no one would be the wiser. But it wouldn't be true. My whole life has been a fraud and I won't see it finish the way it began that day in the bus station.

The truth is, I believed my mother had abandoned me. It had been clear to me for some time that I was the result of some indiscretion. And from the comments I'd overheard in the neighborhood, I knew my mother was considered soiled goods. Weigh in the fact that we lived in an area notably bereft of prospective suitors, and that her maternal instincts were haphazard at best, and you could conclude that my mother saw me as a burden on her future. Or at least, that's what I thought as I stood there in the spring sun. If I had been a better boy— smarter, better-behaved, tidier, something—then perhaps she would have kept me. But I wasn't, so she had arranged for me to be dropped off in a strange town, with a few clothes in a cheap suitcase. It was her judgment of my worth, and there was no appeal.

Sitting there on the bench, I didn't consciously decide not to talk to anyone. At first I was just stunned. For the first hour, I was alone, so there was no one to talk to. By the time Jenkins, the station manager, came outside and spotted me, fright and loneliness had set in.

"Your folks are a little late getting here, huh?" he said. "Did they know what time your bus was due in?"

I stared at him, but kept quiet. He was a rumpled, bear-sized fellow, friendly and with a deliberate calm about him. He settled onto the bench next to me.

"How about a sucker?" he said. When I didn't respond, he drew a lollipop from his pocket and held it in front of my face. I hadn't eaten since the day before, so I unwrapped it and popped it in my mouth.

We sat together for a few minutes, me working the sucker and Jenkins idly scanning the street beyond the parking lot. After a while he slapped his knee and stood, saying, "Well, I've got to get back to work."

We regarded each other for a moment; then he said, "Come in and let me know when your folks get here, OK?" When I didn't say anything, a puzzled look crossed his face. He shrugged and went back inside the station.

A few minutes later, another bus pulled in and for the next hour the station was busy. People bustled about, luggage was stacked near my bench, and the lunch counter inside did a brisk business. When things subsided, I saw Jenkins poke his head out the door and look in my direction, but that time he, too, was silent. He withdrew back inside and I sat alone for a long time. There was a quiver in my stomach that I couldn't control. A few times it spread throughout my body, causing me to shake all over until I tucked my hands under my thighs and mashed my knees together. Controlling it seemed very important to me. If I couldn't stop myself from shaking, then I wouldn't be able to stop myself from crying. And I had it fixed in my head that if I simply sat quietly, without making a sound, somehow things would right themselves.

Otherwise, I had no idea what to do. Fiction is full of boys who, when cast adrift in the world, pole themselves down the Mississippi River on a raft or fall in with treasure seekers and run afoul of pirates, having adventures at every turn before finding their way home again. If God were a novelist, it would have been different for me: I would have signed on as an animal attendant with the circus, discovered the lion tamer was an escaped murderer, foiled his plan to rob the manager of the circus receipts, and been reunited at center ring with my mother, who—after a mixup at a bus depot sent us in opposite directions—had searched frantically for me for weeks, pausing only once long enough to take in a circus performance.

But God is a forgetful sort. He puts events into motion, then lets his attention be diverted by a typhoon in the Bay of Bengal or something, and never remembers leaving a little boy alone in a bus station somewhere in Georgia. I suppose that's what happens when you've got the whole universe to tend to. Your attention strays and things go awry. How else do you explain Richard Nixon?

◆ ◆ ◆

I became officially deaf when the policeman appeared.

The morning passed with me rooted to the bench. Two other buses arrived and disgorged their passengers, which kept the station busy until noon. At one point I heard Jenkins say in my direction, "Do you want something to eat?" but I was busy with my shakes right then, so I ignored him.

It's reasonable to ask why I didn't simply explain the situation to someone and get help, instead of squatting on that bench and refusing to talk. I've wondered myself many times. But sometimes at night, as I lie on my cot in the storage room, I can still remember how suffocating my panic felt that morning. When we boarded the bus, my mother hadn't mentioned where we were going, so I had no idea what our destination was. I had no idea where I was when I woke up. My only known relative in the world had vanished, and I believed it was all my fault.

In the first few hours, I must have felt that my silence could somehow stop time, that my refusal to acknowledge anyone made the situation less real. And in the days that followed, I learned to like being deaf. Once people concluded I couldn't hear, they carried on with their business around me. It was like being in a bubble that allowed everything in except emotion.

When the sun was high in the sky, Jenkins reappeared with another man. They stood together at the far end of the bench, talking and nodding in my direction as I watched them. The other man wore a uniform with a patch on the shirt that said "Barrington Police Department."

"He got off the first bus this morning and has been sitting there ever since," Jenkins said. "I don't think anybody's coming for him."

"Was he alone on the bus?" the policeman asked.

"The driver wasn't sure, but he thinks so. It was the bus from Birmingham, and he picked it up last night from the other driver. He doesn't remember seeing anyone else with the boy, and when he counted heads, he had the right number of tickets."

The policeman considered this for a moment, then said, "What's the kid say when you ask him about it?"

"He won't say a word," Jenkins replied. "I believe he might be deaf."

The policeman grunted and walked the length of the bench toward me. Looking down, he demanded: "What's your name, boy?"

This was my first encounter with law enforcement and it was shaping up poorly. The officer was a rough-looking sort, with sweat stains under his arms and swollen, callused fingers that looked like they'd been broken and not set properly. He seemed resentful, as if I had imposed on his time. In later years, he would gain minor fame for being one of the few police officers ever convicted in the South for assaulting a Negro in custody. He spent two years in the state prison in Reidsville for that little venture into race relations.

When I didn't answer, he gave a snort of frustration and walked back to Jenkins. "Stand him up with his back to me," the policeman instructed.

Jenkins came over and tugged on my arm until I stood. When I heard the policeman's creaky leather belt right behind me, I knew what was coming.

"YAAAAAH!" he shouted, just a few inches from the back of my head. I didn't move.

The two of them withdrew once again to the far end of the bench. "OK, he's deaf," the cop said. "What the devil do you want me to do about it?"

◆ ◆ ◆

For the rest of his life, Jenkins still talked to me. Even though no one disputed the policeman's pronouncement of my deafness—it was taken as gospel from that moment—Jenkins still chattered away at me for years. At first, I wondered if he hoped to trick me into revealing that I could hear after all. Eventually, though, I noticed that nothing Jenkins said required an answer. He was just talking himself through the care and feeding of a deaf orphan.

The policeman's visit ended inconclusively. He and Jenkins quibbled awhile—Jenkins saying I certainly looked abandoned, the cop replying that someone eventually would be along for me—and he left with a vague promise to come by later to check on me. I remained sitting on the bench.

At midafternoon, Jenkins brought a sandwich and a glass of milk. "You're probably starved," he said. "I can't let you sit here all day without eating. Finish this up, then I'll bring you some pie."

I was indeed hungry. My mother had packed some food from the kitchen at home and we'd eaten on the bus the night before, but that seemed like a long time ago. I gobbled the sandwich down and drained the milk. A few minutes later, Jenkins returned with a slice of blackberry pie.

By late afternoon, it was apparent the station was closing up. I could see chairs being stacked on tables in the snack bar and an elderly black man was sweeping up the parking lot. My mother's suitcase and a remaining box from the freight delivery were taken inside, with no one making the connection between me and this stray bag. From inside the station, I could hear an interior door being opened and the sound of boxes being pushed along the floor.

The policeman never returned, probably being too busy in Buttermilk Bottom spreading good cheer. Just before dusk, Jenkins came outside and sat on the bench beside me.

"Looks like your folks aren't going to make it today," he said. "I keep a cot in the storeroom. You can stay there for the night. I'm sure somebody will turn up tomorrow."

Thus, for the second evening in a row, someone had predicted the following day would arrive with new promise. In my mother's case, she was right: everything was different the next day. In Jenkins's case, he was wrong. No one turned up, and the storeroom became my home.

He tugged at my elbow and led me in. He pantomimed turning the lights off, then waved good night. When I was sure he was gone, I crept out to the waiting area and looked for my mother's suitcase, searching behind the ticket counter and underneath desks. I couldn't find it anywhere. More than twenty years passed before I came across it, and when I did, everything changed yet again.

4 I was already awake when Jenkins stuck his head in the storeroom early on my second morning in Barrington. "Do you want something to eat?" he asked, putting one hand, palm up, in front of his face and making scooping motions with the other, an exaggerated pantomime of eating that he accompanied with gobbling noises. I had to laugh.

"See? Things are looking up. Let's get breakfast," he said, giving me a come-along wave of his arm.

We walked to the station's waiting area and headed for the lunch counter located at the far end. Jenkins directed me to one of the stools, then went behind the counter and shouted through the window to the kitchen, "C'mon, Lucille, you've got a hungry customer here."

After a moment, a woman wearing a cook's apron came out and gave me a close look. "Is this him?" she asked.

"Yes, and just because he's deaf doesn't mean he doesn't understand things," Jenkins said. "So just be your normal unpleasant self. He'll catch on soon enough."

"I'll make him some breakfast, but it's going on your tab. Chickens don't lay for free."

"Your chickens finally get unionized? I told you that would happen if you didn't treat them better."

The woman snorted and disappeared into the kitchen. A few minutes later, she returned with a plate of bacon and eggs and set it in front of me, then went back to the kitchen. Jenkins joined her, and as I ate, I could hear the two of them talking.

"What are you going to do if no one comes for him today?"

"I don't know exactly. I don't want to call the police again. It ain't a crime to be lost from your family, but he'll sure be treated like a criminal if they take him."

"Where's he from?"

"I haven't asked him yet. He was on the bus from Birmingham, but it makes at least a dozen stops before it gets here. He could have gotten on anywhere. But I don't think it will help much to know," he said.

"Why not?"

"Think about it. Any other lost kid would have been blubbering and crying, but he wasn't. He looked scared, but he didn't write out his name or town or anything."

"Maybe he doesn't know how to write," Lucille said. "Maybe the only way he knows how to say anything is with that finger talk dummies use."

"I doubt it. You can see in his eyes he's a bright kid. I get the feeling he just doesn't have anything to go back to."

They fell quiet. I finished my eggs, and put the knife and fork together in the middle of the plate. I slid off the stool, went around to the other side of the counter, and put the plate onto the shelf below the window to the kitchen. Then I returned to my seat.

Lucille came to the window, gave me a sly wink, and took the plate.

"What are you going to do with him?" she asked again.

"We'll see," Jenkins said.

◆ ◆ ◆

The station got busy quickly and I was left on my own for most of the morning. After straightening up the cot and splashing my face with cold water from a sink I found tucked away in an alcove, I resumed my spot on the bench outside.

The sun was still low in a cloudless sky, but announced its intention to make that spring day unseasonably hot. A bus was parked in one of the bays, its driver making his way down the aisle between the seats, tossing trash through open windows. I looked around, spotted a trash barrel at the corner of the station's lot, and dragged it over to the bus. I picked up the trash being thrown out, then sorted through the boxes of freight and stray suitcases that had been left in a jumble against the wall. I set the bags neatly together and stacked the boxes.

I kept busy. Whenever I stopped to rest, my mother crowded her way into my thoughts, so I would look for another chore. There was lots to do. The Barrington bus depot seemed to be a magnet for windblown trash. My ten-year-old's mind decided that it must have been due to its look: a concrete-block structure painted white, with a flat roof and pavement all around, apparently designed by someone who thought prisons were flamboyant and frivolous. If buildings send out messages, here was the bus station's: "Got a box of take-out chicken scraps you don't know what to do with? Throw them in my parking lot! And piss against the wall while you're here!"

At one point in the morning, I noticed Jenkins watching me from the doorway. I waved, which brought a broad grin. A few moments later, I saw that Lucille had joined him; they stood together watching me pick up trash.

At midday, I stopped and returned to the bench to rest. Almost immediately, Jenkins came out with a sandwich, as if he'd been waiting for me to stop. "You're a busy little cricket," he said, handing me the plate.

I can't say when things shifted—when I stopped being a lost boy and started being part of the landscape—but that moment can lay as much claim as any. Almost imperceptibly, Jenkins signaled a change. He didn't linger, after giving me the sandwich, with that quizzical what-do-I-do-now? look on his face. And the bench had taken on a comfortable feel.

But most of all, my stomach no longer knotted when I remembered the way I felt when I'd gotten off the bus the day before. I hadn't forgotten it, mind you; but panic had been replaced with deadness. My range of reactions had been narrowed. Silence kept my emotions at bay in those early days when I surely otherwise would have started crying and never stopped. But I never recovered those emotions. I've spent the last fifty years with essentially the same expression on my face.

Jenkins seemed content to just let me work around the bus station, but one morning a few days later, as I sat eating breakfast, Lucille brought up school.

"You can't keep him out of class to work around here," she said. "He ain't some sharecropper's son."

Jenkins bristled at that. "I don't tell him to work. You see him. From the time that boy gets up in the morning, he's doing something. Am I supposed to tell him to stop?"

"It ain't right. If you're gonna get the benefit of his work, then you've got to tend to him," she said.

"He sweeps up over here, too. This old roach hotel of yours is looking a lot tidier these days."

"That's right, he does, and I've been feeding him three meals a day. So now it's your turn. You'd better get him enrolled in school. Eventually, somebody's gonna come hunting him, and it will look a damn sight better if you've done something other than treat him like a slave."

The next day, after the morning bus to Atlanta had rolled

out, Jenkins took me to Barrington Elementary School. We were pointed to the principal's office, and after a ten-minute wait outside we were ushered into the presence of Gladys Harrison. If life hadn't already scared me into silence, Gladys could have done the job.

A middle-aged spinster who lived with her mother, Miss Harrison was a tall, beaky, angular woman who wore sensible shoes and a high-necked blouse pinned at the throat with a cameo. She was all elbows and nose, and she rarely stopped moving, flapping and pecking her way around the office. Her manner matched her appearance: brusque and businesslike, with lots of sharp edges in unexpected places.

"You're Jenkins, right? From the bus station?" she asked.

"Yes ma'am," he said. "And this is . . ."

"And who's this young man?" she asked, cutting Jenkins off and making clear he was expected to answer the question, no more.

"His name is Sammy Ayers."

"Relative of yours?"

"No one knows who he is. He just appeared."

She had already begun to fill out an enrollment form, but that brought her up short.

"He just appeared where?"

"Here. In Barrington. At the bus station."

"Where's he from?"

"He says he's from Birmingham, Alabama."

"What do you mean he just appeared?"

"He got off one of the early buses several mornings ago. He was alone and apparently lost. I've been tending to him ever since and I thought he should be in school while we wait for things to get sorted out."

Miss Harrison fixed a fierce gaze on me and said, "Young man, what the devil is going on? Where are your parents?"

"There's one other thing, ma'am," Jenkins said. "It seems that he's a deaf-mute."

"A deaf-mute," she repeated.

"He hasn't uttered a word. He's stone-deaf."

"I thought you said he told you he was from Birmingham."

"He wrote his name and hometown on a paper for me." At Lucille's prodding a couple of days earlier, Jenkins had asked me to write down every detail that could help authorities get me home. I'd simply written my name, and noted that I lived in Birmingham near the mill. I didn't know how to explain that I'd been abandoned.

"Have you called the police?"

"I did. An officer came by and said to give it a few days, somebody'd come looking for him."

"He's not a kitten. You can't just set out a dish of milk and adopt him. Something's got to be done."

"Yes ma'am, I know that. But do you think it's best to turn him over to the police and courts just now?"

"They're equipped to handle something like this," she said.

"They'll do the same thing we're doing, only with more fuss. If you can get him enrolled, I can make sure the police keep trying to track down his folks."

I could sense Miss Harrison's resolve weakening. "Has he got somewhere to stay?"

"I've fixed him up a place."

She looked back at me and put her hands together, palms up, like she was holding a book. "Can you read?" she asked.

When I nodded, she said, "Well, let's see if we can figure out what grade he's supposed to be in. I don't have anyone who knows about teaching the deaf, but it won't hurt to let him sit in class."

◆ ◆ ◆

The first of dozens of teachers to assign me to the back of the class was Mrs. Bracey, in whose care I finally was placed. She was the overseer of an unruly fourth grade, and I suspect that Miss Harrison's placement was practical rather than academic: she figured the noise wouldn't bother me.

I wasn't there long. I'd arrived in Barrington in the spring and there were only six weeks of school left. But that was long enough for one towhead to make me the target of his torment.

"A dummy, huh?" he said as I took the desk next to his. Mrs. Bracey evidently had been given the chance to prepare her class for the arrival of this exotic creature. "I'll bet I can make those ears ring," he said. With that, he reached over and popped my ear with a rubber band stretched between his fingers and drawn back with his thumb. It hurt like the dickens, causing me to yelp and clap my hand over my ear. It was the first sound I'd made in days, and my own voice sounded foreign to me.

"You heard that, didn't you?" the boy said. Mrs. Bracey— busy writing an assignment on the chalkboard—hadn't even slowed at the commotion. The other children were turned to watch, their faces set with the rapt, feral expressions youngsters get when torture is being perpetrated on someone else.

"Hey," the boy said, and jabbed me in the ribs. "Let's hear you holler again. I'll have you talking in no time." I circled my waist with one arm and kept the other hand cupped over my ear, watching my tormentor for a clue as to what was coming next. He stretched one arm toward the side of my head, reaching the edge of my vision, and when I turned to keep it in sight, he slapped me soundly on the cheek with the other hand. I jumped in fright, prompting the other children to break into laughter.

That finally got Mrs. Bracey's attention. She turned from the chalkboard and peered toward the back of the class. "Tolly, stop joshing with your new friend. You two can play together outside later."

Such was my introduction to Tolliver Tynan, child of privilege, future man of God, and my lifelong nemesis.

I don't know that Jenkins ever nudged the police even once, despite his pledge to Miss Harrison. Instead, the school year concluded, along with Tolliver's daily exhibitions of friendship, and I settled into a routine at the bus station. Jenkins rousted me early every morning and together we had breakfast at Lucille's lunch counter. Then, as he manned the ticket window and generally tended to schedules and the telephone, I worked outside as the luggage wrangler, pulling bags out from underneath the buses and piling them up neatly, taking care to avoid oily spots on the ground.

I also fell into the habit of vigil. As each bus arrived—and I came to know the schedules to the minute—I would sit on the same bench where I spent my first day in Barrington and scan the face of every woman who disembarked. I held out hope that one day my mother would simply step off the bus and reclaim me. Several times during that summer, I thought I saw her, and would fix on a face and wait for the sure click of recognition. It never came, of course. Invariably, the woman's gaze would sweep by me without hesitation. As the weeks went on and thousands of faces paraded by my bench, I became less and less sure that I knew what my mother looked like. The details were sharp: I could remember perfectly her nose and hands and the cast of her eyes, for instance; I still can to this day. But they were like close-up snapshots that you can look at anytime, not a picture of a whole person. That image grew fuzzier by the day. One morning toward the end of the summer, I realized that perhaps the same thing had happened to her, that her memory of me had started to fade. I began crying, and Lucille came out from her kitchen and sat down beside me, cradling my head against her bosom and making gentle shushing noises.

"Well, cricket," she said, "maybe you can't talk, but you sure enough can cry."

At midday, Jenkins would wave me in for lunch. Lucille generally had a pot of soup going, from which she would dip a bowl for me and serve it with the crust ends of bread that she wouldn't give to paying customers. When Jenkins ate with me, we sat together at the counter; otherwise I ate in the kitchen, sitting on a stool pulled up to the shelf just below the serving window.

After lunch, I would begin straightening up the station. Barrington wasn't a hub for the bus line, meaning it wasn't a transfer point for drivers or a place where maintenance was performed on the buses. It was strictly for arrivals and departures, and as such, it tended to be busiest during the middle of the day. By midafternoon, I could begin plucking cigarette butts out of the sanded ashtrays and collecting empty soft-drink bottles that had rolled under the seats. Someone always left a newspaper about, too, so that summer was the start of my lifelong habit of reading the paper every day.

Lucille only served breakfast and lunch, so she closed up by four o'clock. She always left dinner for me on a plate covered by a dish towel, which—when set on a rack inside the just-turned-off oven where she baked bread and pies—stayed warm for hours. I ate while Jenkins finished up in his office, then rinsed the dishes and left them in the bottom of the sink.

For an hour or two before I went to sleep and Jenkins went home, we read. I went through the paper I'd found, while Jenkins put his feet up on his desk and buried his nose in a book. Sometime between eight and nine o'clock, Jenkins would shut his book, look at me, and say, "C'mon, Sambo, it's time to give me a break from your chatter," putting his palms together and laying them on the side of his head. He would watch as I brushed my teeth with baking soda and splashed water on my face, then turn aside discreetly as I stripped off my pants and shirt and crawled into bed. After giving me a wave, Jenkins would leave, snapping lights off around the building as he went.

Those moments before sleep were always the worst. Another day had gone by without my mother coming for me. Occasionally, I wondered if I shouldn't simply leave and go back to Birmingham, to try to find our apartment and see if my mother was there. But I knew no good would come of it. Either she wouldn't be there, and I'd be stuck without someone like Jenkins to keep track of me, or she would be there, which would mean she had set out to abandon me. Little wonder that the scab over my soul grew to its thickest that summer.

Near the end of August, Lucille made sure Jenkins knew what he had to do. "Just keep an eye on the paper, it'll tell you when the first day of class is," she said. "Take him down there that day and register him."

Indeed, two weeks later the *Barrington Chronicle* announced that school was to begin that morning. So Jenkins, after shouting to Lucille to keep an ear cocked for the phone, led me to the school office and found Miss Harrison. She stared at us blankly for a moment before something in her memory registered.

"He's still here," she said.

"Still here," Jenkins confirmed.

"He did all right last year, if I remember. Stand still a moment. I'll be right back."

She disappeared into another office, then came back a minute later carrying a folder open in front of her. "Smart boy. Mrs. Bracey says he paid attention in class and did well on tests. I think we can move him up to the fifth grade. Leave him with me."

Jenkins looked at me and mouthed, "OK?" When I nodded, he thanked Miss Harrison and left hastily. I think he was afraid that if he dallied, she'd have him standing in front of a chalkboard writing "I will not adopt stray children" one hundred times.

She pointed to a chair and I sat down while she flapped off. A few minutes later she returned and took me down the hall to a classroom, where a teacher waited outside.

"His name is Sammy Ayers," Miss Harrison said. "As long as you talk directly to him, he seems to understand well enough. Don't let him slow the class down, though. It's not as if the state is giving us extra funds for the education of the deaf."

The teacher led me inside. The class had grown unruly while we stood in the hall, but it quieted as we entered. From the back of the room I heard a familiar voice.

"He was in my class last year," Tolliver called out. "He can sit here next to me."

As you read on, you might conclude that this remembrance is an extended exercise in score settling, insofar as it regards Tolliver. That's not the purpose; it's just one of the benefits.

My first few years in Barrington were marked by countless slights and pranks at Tolliver's hand. I was fair game. I've always been small, I had few friends, and I tended to do better in class than Tolliver, even though every teacher put me in the back of the room and ignored me. And I never sought relief by complaining to adults. Being abandoned by my mother and having an evil-spirited hooligan crowd into my life both seemed like part of the same celestial plan. My role was not to prevail but to merely endure.

I could detail all the outrages, large and small—the tacks in my chair, the pencils snapped in half, the wet willies in my ear—but one example will do. I'll tell you about the radio.

For a time one year, when we were older, Tolliver and his crowd took to hanging around Lucille's lunch counter for the hour or so between the end of school and her closing. There was no reason for their choice of that location, aside from normal teenage restlessness; it was a place to gather that was different from the previous place to gather. I kept out of sight while he was around, busying myself in the station's back rooms. Jenkins was oblivious, but Lucille noticed.

"I can tell you don't like that boy," she said one day after Tolliver left. "Well, you know what? Neither do I. He's a good-looking kid, but there's something off-center about him."

The radio had arrived as freight one afternoon and remained unclaimed for weeks. They were bulky in those days before transistors, but this was one of the new tabletop models that were beginning to show up in stores. The packing slip indicated it was to be held for pickup at the Barrington bus depot, but eventually Jenkins got tired of tripping over it.

"I'm ready to hang a For Sale sign on this thing," he said as he pushed the crate under his desk. It would sit there until he decided it cramped his legs, then be pushed back into the aisle. This routine had already been played out several times.

I pointed at the box, then tapped myself on the chest. "You want it?" Jenkins asked. I nodded.

He lifted the crate to the top of the desk and we began unpacking it. Lucille, leaning against the lunch counter, called out across the deserted depot, "Are y'all finally doing something with that radio?"

"Sammy says he wants it," Jenkins answered. At precisely that moment, Tolliver and his gang walked in. In a glance, he figured out what was going on.

"A dummy with a radio," he crowed. "What's he going to do? Turn it up real loud and put his ear close to it?"

I picked up the radio and took it to the storeroom where I slept. I knew it was a bit of a risk—it looked strange to see a deaf-mute with a radio—but I hoped it would be passed off as a decorating quirk. Over the few years of my residency, the storeroom had become cluttered with things I'd gathered; an unplugged radio sitting on a shelf would be just another bauble. I set it near the head of my cot, and that night after Jenkins had closed up the station, I plugged the radio in and turned the volume low. I kept it on all night, the music and an-nouncers' voices murmuring in my ear as I slept, a gentle and soothing sound that carried the hint of order and peace in far-away places. I was careful the next morning to unplug it and coil the cord.

I knew Jenkins would forget about the radio as soon as it was out of sight. But I should have guessed that Tolliver wouldn't.

The day after we unpacked the radio, Jenkins sent me to the post office to mail a package. When I returned, Tolliver and his pals were settled in at Lucille's counter. "How's the ra-dio work, Sammy?" Tolliver asked as I went by. His friends smirked.

Tolliver already knew the answer, but I didn't find out un-til that evening, when I settled in my cot. I plugged the radio in and reached up to turn it on, but nothing happened. I jiggled the plug. Nothing. When I sat up and tipped the radio forward to see if the cord had worked loose, I heard pieces sliding around inside and saw scratches on the bottom of the wood cabinet. I knew then that one of them, probably on the pretext of using the depot's rest room—which was off the same corridor as my storeroom—had come in while I was gone and wrecked my radio by slamming it down a few times. It was a perfect bit of mischief. How would a dummy know that his radio didn't work any longer?

This is where I'm supposed to declare that I swore vengeance on Tolliver at that moment. I could pretend that I spent the next twenty years or so plotting my revenge, and no one would be the wiser. But the truth is, I did nothing. Even when I got the opportunity to even things up with him, chance—in the form of John Lennon, the young preacher Perry Ray Pruitt, and a nameless, alcoholic highway department bureaucrat—played the biggest part. In fact, my revenge took the same form as my life itself: a giant deceit, known but to one person. In both cases, that one person was an elderly black man named Archibald Thacker.

Actually, the worst thing Tolliver ever did to me wasn't intentional.

One afternoon almost a year after I arrived in Barrington, I found something waiting for me at the bus depot. I'd run an errand for Jenkins after school, and when I returned Lucille waved me over to her lunch counter.

"Somebody left this for you," she said, pushing an envelope across the countertop. Her tone was bemused. "A girl."

The envelope was heavy and red, and on its front was a doe-eyed cupid with an arrow notched into his bow. For a moment, it didn't register; then I remembered it was Valentine's Day. Earlier, at school, my classmates had traded valentines, the sort that are sold to children by dime stores and carry simple messages like "Be Mine" and "I'm Yours." For a half hour, they had flitted around the classroom in a chaotic ballet, dropping valentines on desks until a small pile of greetings had collected on each one. The teacher made a great show of putting one from her on my desk, and a pair of others were dropped there by children whose attentive mothers had made sure no one was overlooked when valentines were prepared the night before. But I had ignored them. I'd forgotten it was Valentine's Day, and didn't have the money even if I'd wanted to buy cards to trade. Besides, what good would a fistful of valentines do the next time I was dropped off alone in a strange town? I could imagine my next encounter with a police officer or bus station manager: "Well, sir, I know it appears I'm a luckless orphan, but as you can see from these valentines, I once was loved by someone, so perhaps you could help me pretend that my mother will be along for me directly."

I felt Lucille watching me. I jammed the card in my pocket and went about my business.

Later, after I'd eaten the dinner Lucille set aside for me, I retrieved the card and sat on my cot to examine it. There was nothing on the envelope to indicate who it was from. Only the tip of the triangular flap had been moistened, so I was able to pop it open with my thumb without ripping the envelope. The valentine was printed on heavy paper and embossed with a message that said, "Thinking of you on this most special of days." Inside, on one of the blank pages, was a second note added by hand: "I'm so glad you're in my class." Beneath that was a signature.

I recognized the name. She was a quiet, pretty girl who sat in the row of desks closest to the window. I'd paid her little note, having devoted most of my time to being alert for Tolliver's next torment. I was bewildered by her attention. I read both inscriptions several times for clues, but found none.

The next morning, before I left for school, Lucille had a surprise of her own for me. "I got this for you yesterday," she said, handing me a flat, brown paper sack. Inside was another valentine, this one unsigned and unsealed, ready to be pressed into service. "I thought you might need it. It wouldn't hurt to be a day late, if you want to give it to someone."

As I ate my breakfast, I thought about what I would write. Then later, just before setting off for school, I scribbled my note: "Thank you for the card. I'll tell my Mom what a nice thing you did when she comes back. Sincerely yours, Samuel Ayers."

Thus began a peculiar ten-year courtship. The next year, the process was repeated, although she didn't deliver it privately; that time, she handed it to me at school, presenting it with a flourish that prompted her friends to titter behind their hands. It was again an expensive, oversized card in a heavy envelope, and the inscription again proclaimed her happiness for my presence. And again, I was a day late with my reply.

The following year, I was prepared. As she approached with yet another large red envelope in hand, I had its twin ready. We exchanged them in the hallway outside the classroom.

"Oh, Sammy, you remembered," she said. I listened hard for sarcasm, but there was none.

For all my puzzlement, I was grateful for the attention. It gave a focus to my year, and by Christmas I usually was already thinking about the card I would get and the one I would offer. But eventually I realized that there was nothing special in her behavior on that day. Alone among my classmates, she treated me in a perfectly ordinary and friendly way all the time. I got the same cheery greeting that everyone else got, the same smile, the same offer to share her cookies at lunch, of which there were always too many for her to eat. As the years went on, she was absolutely consistent: while my classmates moved from curiosity about me to disdain to contempt as they grew, I remained to her just another boy in her class. It was the kindest thing anyone could have done.

I was in love with her, of course. I devoted days to crafting the message I would write in her card, then would spend days afterwards rereading hers to me to make sure some nuance didn't escape me. My notes to her were always proper and even a bit detached. I was afraid that a too heartfelt message would scare her away, would send her scampering back to her kind and their I-told-you-so scoldings about the pitfalls of mixing with boys like me: parentless, bus station–dwelling, friendless, deaf and dumb. So I wrote my notes and hoped she would somehow know my ache. It was the closest thing to a romance I ever had, and as with any romance, there was a mystery at the center. I never learned why she chose me to get a special valentine.

Perhaps she would have told me someday, had Tolliver not killed her.

Yes, I hated him. Tolliver was a thief and a bully. He was convicted of being the first and immortalized on film as being the second. He came to be reviled in the town that once revered him, and his name became synonymous with moral treachery.

Ironically, I think the court of public opinion was unfair. Everyone knew what Tolliver was like from his childhood on, yet it didn't seem to matter. For most of his life, people focused on his good qualities: He was personable and voluble, and after he became a preacher, his looks of concern were so sincere that his parishioners were comforted by a single furrowing of his brow. If he was also a rogue and a dandy, you didn't mind because his well-practiced good nature invited you in on the joke, and that acknowledgment of inconsistency was part of his charm.

It was only after the events of August 1966 that people put a different twist on these things. What had seemed like minor character flaws took on a sinister quality, and were cited as proof of psychopathy. As glad as I was to see it happen, I knew it wasn't warranted. Tolliver was like anyone else. He obtained his job through deceit, milked it for power and prestige, and lunged after the prospect of a quick profit like a bass goes after a cricket.

This is perfectly ordinary behavior in the business world, and please don't try my patience by proclaiming that running a church isn't business. It most assuredly is. The only difference is that you work weekends.

So I suppose I've always resented that people climbed aboard my private hate wagon. I despised Tolliver for reasons that had nothing to do with anyone else. You'll have to find Elmer Gantry somewhere else. I won't serve him to you here.

5

People occasionally tell deaf-mutes things they would never otherwise talk about. It's not as absurd as it sounds. Granted, the deaf-mute can't hear what's being said, but the speaker usually is talking to himself anyway. It's the best kind of therapy: you can unburden yourself without having a shrink ask you what it felt like to see your mother naked.

Years after I arrived in Barrington, Jenkins told me a remarkable story. I'll repeat it here, because it helps answer an obvious question: Why did a man who was so kind to me otherwise let me live in a bus station all my life?

He told it on a Christmas Day in the early 1950s. I was grown by then, and starting to establish myself as a hand for hire. Only a few buses were running, and the station was deserted most of the day. Jenkins had spent the afternoon away, and when he returned, I was sitting at the lunch counter thumbing through a newspaper. He took the stool next to me and started talking.

"You didn't know I was married, did you? You didn't know

that I once had a wife and a daughter and a little farm. You probably think that all I've ever done is run this bus station, right?" I shrugged.

"Well, that's not so. I was a farmer. I owned a little land that I'd gotten from my daddy. I farmed until the day I realized my life was going to be just like his. I was going to grub around in the same tired dirt, borrowing from the same bank each year to buy the same seeds and supplies. And have nothing left over when I paid it back. I was taking a break one afternoon, sitting in the shade and thinking that it was getting toward the end of summer and I could tell already it was going to be a rotten year. I was twenty-two years old. I didn't have much schooling and I'd never been out of Soque County. I sat there and realized that if I didn't do something about it, my kids would be sitting under that same tree in twenty years. Wondering why there wasn't something else to life.

"So I joined the Army. My wife was upset and worried that they would starve, but I told her I would send all my money home and that she could keep a garden to help with food. I told her I was desperate to learn something, to be something. It was 1918 and the war seemed like an adventure. I didn't read newspapers then, I had no idea what it was like. But I got it fixed in my head that coming home in two years in a fine uniform with a few medals was going to get me off that farm and into a nice job. At a bank or something.

"Well, I got as far as Camp Dix, New Jersey, before the armistice was signed. A few days later a rumor went around that the newest of us were going to be mustered out early. They said that because there wasn't a war going on anymore, they didn't need all these soldiers. So some of us would be shipped home. At least, that's what the rumor was.

"I'd fallen in with a bunch of guys, most of them dirt-diggers like me. But a couple of them weren't. One of them was an

47

Irish kid from New York City, named Cork. He saw that I was unhappy with the notion that I was just going to end up back at that farm, so he said, 'You want an adventure? Let's go into the city this weekend.'

"We both had leave coming, so I agreed. When Friday came, we got into clean clothes and asked the captain to sign the passes that would get us back through the gate. Then we set off. I had all my money with me. I'd been sending money home all along, but keeping just a little bit back, so I had eleven dollars in my pocket.

"I was pretty excited to see New York City and I wasn't disappointed. Camp Dix was about sixty miles away, so it took us a while to get there, hitching rides and all. You've never seen such buildings and people in your life. If Cork hadn't been with me, I'd have been lost. The delivery truck we hitched with dropped us off just as we got over a big bridge into the city proper, but Cork knew how to figure the trolleys. He said we were going downtown, although it all looked downtown to me. I had no idea where we ended up. I stayed close to Cork. We got something to eat first, then started going from saloon to saloon. This was still a year or so before Prohibition, so it was all out in the open.

"Cork seemed to know people in every place, and he was showing off a bit, talking too loud and calling me 'Georgia boy' in front of everyone. He wasn't being mean about it. He was just the way people get when they've had too much to drink and think they're better friends with you than they really are."

At the time, I wondered why Jenkins was telling me this tale. Normally a good-spirited fellow, he was morose that day, delivering his words in a flat, expressionless tone. The station remained deserted, and the stillness only emphasized his mournful tone. I was puzzled why the story of a couple of soldiers getting drunk in New York City prompted such gravity. I soon found out.

"At one point, he asked if I wanted to see a show. 'A Broadway show?' I asked. He laughed and repeated my question to the bartender, who also laughed. They made me feel stupid. The places we'd visited had kept getting darker and dirtier, and this place was the worst. You had to walk down a flight of steps from the street to get to it. And once you got there, it was hot and smelly and crowded. It was full of service guys like me and Cork. They all seemed to be drunk.

"We had to give the bartender five dollars each for the show. I thought that was a lot, and I said so. But Cork told me to shut up and pay the man. It was if he'd suddenly gotten tired of me. We went down a hallway in the back to a door where a guy stood. Cork told him we'd paid Ernie, and the guy nodded and opened the door. There were about three dozen chairs, all of them turned to face what looked like one of those tables you see in a doctor's office, that you lie down on to get examined. Most of the chairs had guys sitting in them, but Cork and I found two near the edge of the room.

"After a while, a man and woman came out from behind a drape along one wall. The man was dressed like a doctor and the woman looked like a showgirl. You know, had a dress cut real low and her bosoms pushed up. Anyway, they talked in these loud, stagey voices, with the woman acting all bashful and saying she had a personal problem, and the doctor trying to get her out of her clothes so he could take a look. I figured I knew what was coming, and sure enough, she eventually took off her dress. Everyone in the room clapped and whistled and generally carried on. I thought that would be the end of it, but it wasn't. She was standing there almost naked, and the doctor told her to strip off her underwear and hop onto the table.

"So she took off the rest and lay down on her back with her feet toward the chairs. Then she drew her knees up and put her feet down flat, so everyone had a clear view of her privates. The room was real quiet then while everyone took this in.

49

G. D. Gearino

They were all younger than me, and it probably was the first time any of them had seen a woman that way. Actually, even though I was married, I can't say I'd seen a woman's privates either. It ain't all that pretty a sight.

"Anyway, the doctor fellow announced that he saw what the problem was. He went over to a little table I hadn't noticed before and picked up a tin, showing it to the audience with a magician's flourish. It was smoked oysters. Then he picks up a long-handled spoon, like the kind they give you with iced tea in fancy restaurants, and takes them over and sets them down on the table, next to her butt. Now this is disgusting and I probably shouldn't say it, but here's what he did. He pushed a bunch of those oysters into her privates and then fished them out with that spoon, one by one, and ate them.

"I felt sick. It was awful, treating a woman like that with all those men watching. I looked at Cork and said, 'This ain't right,' but he didn't say anything. He just kept staring. I said, 'I'm leaving,' but he still didn't say anything, so I pushed my way out of the room and left.

"I had no idea where I was, but I walked in the direction we'd come. I remembered the name of the bridge we'd crossed to get into the city, so a couple of times I asked someone where it was. Even late at night, there were thousands of people out. I felt light-headed and every few blocks I had to stop and take a deep breath. Eventually I found the bridge and crossed it, then began looking for a ride back to the base. By the time I got a lift on a supply truck, I was sick and dizzy. I couldn't draw a good breath and felt hot all over. All I could think about was getting back to the base and crawling into my bunk. Even as fevered as I was, I kept imagining myself lying down with a blanket pulled over me for warmth. That truck seemed to take the whole night, and when I finally got dropped off near the base, I didn't make it any farther than the guardhouse before I collapsed.

50

"Have you heard of the Spanish flu?" Jenkins asked. I shook my head. "Well, it hit in 1918 and killed two hundred thousand people in one month. And that's just in this country. I read somewhere that it may have killed twenty million people around the world. They say it was the greatest plague ever, even worse than the Black Death. Well, I had that flu.

"They took me to the base hospital, where they had a whole ward full of guys with the flu. A lot of them died, I later found out. I was in real bad shape. There were times when I was awake, but most of the time I was in some crazy, feverish place. Once, I heard the doctor tell a Negro orderly to move me off to the corner of the ward and stay with me until I died. He did, too, except of course I didn't die. He and another Negro sat with me a long time. I could hear them talking sometimes. And in my worst moments, I could feel one of them wipe my face and say things in my ear to calm me down. They were kinder to me than I'll bet any white stranger had ever been to them. I never forgot that.

"It took several weeks for me to recover. I spent hours lying in that hospital bed, staring at the wall and thinking about things. I concluded that getting sick was God's punishment. I had behaved badly. I'd gotten too proud to be a farmer. I'd abandoned my family just because I'd gotten restless. And I'd witnessed the evil use of a woman's body. That seemed like the worst one. I knew something was going to happen when we sat down in that back room. I knew it was going to involve a woman being naked, but I stayed anyway. And as I lay there in that hospital bed, I made myself admit that up until that last part, I had liked it. I liked seeing her naked. There's a part of every man that's best left quiet, but I had let it be stirred up. That was my worst sin, and I thanked God I wasn't dead. That I had another chance. But I found out he wasn't done with me yet.

"Of course, I wasn't much use to the Army after being sick, so I got mustered out after all. By mid-December, I was on a train back home, just four months after I'd left.

"It was a wonderful reunion. The doctor had written my wife that I was badly sick and might die. And I don't think the letters I wrote after that eased her mind much. When I arrived, I could see she'd been terribly worried. Even my daughter treated me like a ghost at first. But it was so sweet. I must have hugged each of them a hundred times. I felt peaceful, and the restlessness that had made me leave in the first place had been burned out of me.

"But I had brought it with me.

"My daughter woke up one morning feverish and trembling. Later on that day, my wife took on a pale look and said she needed to rest a bit. They got worse by the hour, and I recognized some of the same things in them I had felt just a few weeks before. I tended to them the best I could, remembering what the army doctor had done for me. I also sent for the doctor in town. Between us, we did everything we could, but they just got worse. They both died on the same day."

Jenkins fell quiet. The only sound was the occasional car passing outside, and the creaks and moans of the station's heating system. We sat in the silence a long time before he spoke again.

"I buried them together, with enough room for me on one side. I can't hurt them next time, being close like that."

You'd think that a man who'd had his family taken from him would feel lucky to get another chance at the love of a child when fate delivers a lost boy to his bus station twenty-two years later. But it wasn't like that. If it had been, Jenkins would have taken me into his home, seen to my education, and treated me like a son. Instead, he let me live in a storeroom and treated me like an employee.

Don't misunderstand me, though. I know I was a strange child, silent and private and detached. I didn't make myself lovable. And I don't think Jenkins was capable of giving me anything more than he did. He recognized me as another wounded soul, and he and Lucille were the closest thing to a family I had. And after hearing his story, I understood his rare, dignified treatment of black folks.

No doubt, Jenkins threw me a line and pulled me into the lifeboat when I first arrived in Barrington. But those peculiar Protestant notions of divine retribution had ensured that the lifeboat didn't have many provisions.

On a hunch, the day after I heard Jenkins's story, I walked to the Barrington cemetery and searched for hours until I found the graves. Sure enough, both had died on December 25, 1918. I knew exactly how he took it: "Watch the naked girl, will you, Jenkins? Here's your Christmas gift."

As it turns out, though, Jenkins did adopt me, after a fashion.

Like bus stations the world over, Barrington's depot has a row of coin lockers in which travelers store luggage for a while. I suspect they work the same everywhere: You jam your bag into the locker, close the door, and drop a quarter into the slot, which allows you to turn the key and remove it from the lock. When you open the locker again, the lock somehow grabs the key and won't let it loose until another quarter is deposited. It's an odd system. The guy who just needs a place to stash a bag long enough to run across the street for a soft drink at the pharmacy pays the same as the guy who stores his bag for years.

The bank of lockers stood just inside the station door, nine in all stacked in three rows of three. It wouldn't have mattered how you numbered them, top to bottom or left to right, locker 9 was destined to be the locker world's stepchild. Not only was it on the bottom row close enough to the floor to demand a squat, it was the locker nearest to the station door, meaning any user ran the risk of being brained if the door was thrown open too vigorously.

But locker 9's user was one of those long-term tenants. Its key had long since disappeared and its door remained locked for years, keeping its contents a mystery. Every once in a while, Jenkins would jiggle the handle and proclaim that he probably should get the locksmith in to pry it open. But the moment always passed and the locker remained shut.

In fact, Jenkins knew exactly what was inside. I suppose he thought it was a safe place to stash my adoption papers.

6 People get the oddest ideas by reading newspapers. They don't realize that newspapers are produced by frustrated, half-talented writers who spend their professional lives in large, noisy rooms, feeding off each other's neuroses and trying to forget that while they hope to change the world, their real function is to report on high school sports, giant vegetables and long-lost pets that have returned home after a cross-country odyssey. I suspect it makes them crazy, or vicious. Or both.

As far as I can tell, your typical small-town newspaper reporter spends most of his day in bars and coffee shops flirting ineptly with waitresses or begging news tips from important people who are invariably better-looking and can shave without cutting themselves. Toward the end of the day, the reporter will rush back to the newsroom to write an account of a council meeting he didn't actually attend, while an editor who has his alcoholic dementia temporarily under control reminds him of deadline with remarks like, "I hope we can expect that piece before the end of the current geologic era." The reporter will turn in the story with the mayor's name misspelled, the editor will add a few mistakes of his own, and the finished product will be thrown on porches all over town.

And people like Perry Ray Pruitt will pick it up and believe everything it contains is true.

Of course, on that fifth day of August 1966 when my story starts, the front-page article that caught Perry Ray's eye was more than true. It was divine. As he headed for Mrs. Maddie Tynan's kitchen, Perry Ray saw that the *Barrington Chronicle* was the Lord's messenger, and that it finally had delivered the miracle for which he had prayed almost ceaselessly for two days.

No one else would have seen a miracle in a simple one-column news report from the Associated Press. But then, no one else was a twenty-one-year-old recent graduate of Barrington Baptist College who had gone halfway through his first summer revival without laying claim to so much as a single baptism. Had the article been on an inside page—which means Perry Ray likely wouldn't have seen it at all because his fetching of the paper, which he rarely read himself, was a courtesy to old Maddie—or had he been able to put a few baptisms on the scoreboard and not arrive at that moment feeling panicky about his future in the ministry, none of this would have happened. Funny, isn't it? History turns because an editor decides that rock 'n' roll is ready for page one, or because a heathen decides to postpone the big step of washing away his sins in the cleansing water of the baptismal font.

Considering that Perry Ray Pruitt and Barrington Baptist Church together became one of the most vivid images of the sixties— largely thanks to *Life* magazine, which put that famous photograph of the two of them on its cover—it helps to know where the church stood, both in town and in the minds of Barrington's citizens.

Along with the courthouse, it bracketed the patch of lawn that is the town square. It was a huge brick structure, with a half-dozen Doric columns across the front, a nave that seated a thousand faithful, and classrooms and offices located in wings that spread from either side of the main building. Soaring above it all was a steeple visible from virtually everywhere in town.

The original structure had been built in the 1850s, then torn down forty years later and replaced with a larger one, which itself was replaced yet again in 1946. It also had undergone an interior renovation just a couple of years prior to this eventful summer, which made Barrington Baptist a marvel of spiritual technology. There were lights on rheostats that could make the church as dim as a sepulcher or bright as day. There was a new pipe organ that could rattle windows a block away. There were intercoms in the classrooms and nursery to ensure no one missed so much as a sigh when Tolliver Tynan began hectoring the faithful over their shortcomings as decent Christians. And, directly behind the pulpit, there was an enormous baptismal font, a four hundred-gallon tub outfitted with an electric pump and water heater. At the end of every service, Tolliver would issue the traditional call to the unsaved; at the moment he saw a hand go up, he would flip a switch under the pulpit, causing the pump to begin filling the font with warm, clean, fresh water.

Before the renovation, a baptismal candidate had to wait for the font to be filled by hand from a garden hose, or—if there was water remaining from a recent baptism—bide time while the crickets, mosquitoes, and other drowned wildlife were screened out. But with the new font, Tolliver had only to keep talking for a few minutes—congratulate the convert on his decision, toss off a few inspirational phrases, and solicit an "Amen" or two—until the pump filled the tank. Thanks to hydraulics and a dose of showmanship, he was the only preacher in town who could deliver a sermon, pass a collection plate, save a soul, and have everyone headed for home by noon, all without breaking stride.

Efficiency contributed to Tolliver's downfall, however. As it turned out, it was entirely too easy to get the font drained and refilled with something else.

Because he set this whole chain of events into motion, it also helps that you understand a few things about Perry Ray Pruitt and what it meant to preach the summer revival at Barrington Baptist Church.

None of us in Barrington knew much about him until later, when the *New York Times*—looking for an angle on the whole matter—sent a writer to spend several weeks digging into his life. At the time, we only knew what we saw: that he was one of those men who, even in their later years, are doomed to be called "boyish," having reached adulthood without life leaving its mark on him. But thanks to the *Times*, it became clear that life had certainly tried to leave its mark. His father was a street preacher who had dedicated his mission to exposing the conspiracy among Jehovah's Witnesses to undermine Christianity—a theory based exclusively on the fact that Witnesses do not put steeples on their churches. The elder Pruitt practiced his craft in Atlanta and Perry Ray often accompanied him on his forays into the downtown business district, where he usually mounted a lamppost or mailbox and shouted his gospel until the nearest merchant called the police.

Perry Ray's mother was equally daft, in an altogether different way. She supported the family with a sales job at a department store, and to all appearances was perfectly ordinary. But she ironed obsessively. Standing at her board with a hot iron in hand, she pressed everything. When Perry Ray got his dollar allowance each Saturday, it was a freshly pressed bill. Each page of the morning paper got a quick swipe before being read. Perry Ray's school papers and his father's pamphlets ("Who's Watching the Watchtower?" was one of the more memorable titles) all caught the hot side of her press. There was nothing she wouldn't iron.

You might reasonably ask how Perry Ray grew up normal under those circumstances. The answer is, he didn't. Oh, he did well in school and graduated at the top of his class at Barrington Baptist College. He did what he was told, memorized what was required, and turned his homework in on time (although a whole generation of teachers was bewildered by the smooth, slightly brittle paper he used). But at no point was he actually required to think, especially at a college where the unofficial motto is "Where Reason and Faith Don't Mix."

I suspect that the part of Perry Ray's mind that thought about things had gone out of business years ago, if only as a defensive measure. If you ask how someone growing up in the care of a couple of certifiable lunatics can be unmarked by life, there's your answer. Perry Ray was like a parrot with facial expressions.

I know that sounds harsh, but I don't mean for it to be. I liked Perry Ray. Given a dozen years or so of psychoanalysis, he probably could have come to grips with himself. Of course, most people don't need help in blaming their shortcomings on their parents—including me, by the way. But the one person I know who legitimately could do so, didn't. No matter. I prefer that my men of God be a little dopey. They do less harm that way.

Each year, Barrington Baptist College's top graduate is invited to lead the summer revival at Barrington Baptist Church, and in 1966 that was Perry Ray. His showing was no surprise; as I said, the college placed little premium on thought or debate. Perry Ray, for instance, could tell his teachers in an instant why the race is not to the swift, nor the battle to the strong, nor bread to the wise, nor riches to the intelligent, nor favor to men of skill. (Because time and chance happeneth to them all. See Ecclesiastes, if you can wrestle a Bible away from your local gospel shouter.) He could recite the Beatitudes flawlessly, and he knew which of the Psalms was the shortest (117) and which was the longest (119). Once, for extra credit, Perry Ray memorized every Who Begat Who in the book of Genesis.

But he struggled at times. Every successful Protestant preacher has no small measure of theatrics in him, yet Perry Ray never quite got it down. When time came for him to pound the pulpit to emphasize a point during practice sermons, he invariably dropped his fist long after he'd finished his sentence, causing the thud to echo ponderously through the college chapel, as displaced as a fart during the Lord's Prayer. Perry Ray was forever lowering his voice when he should have shouted and shouting when he should have whispered. And worst of all for a preacher in a church that practices full-immersion baptisms, he repeatedly dunked baptismal candidates without first pinching their noses shut as he pushed them backwards into the water, causing them to come up in the first moment of their new spiritual lives coughing and sputtering.

"Perry Ray," a teacher said at one point, "we can't have folks coming to Jesus with a belly full of water. You've got to pinch their noses shut, or you'll be working overtime preaching funerals for people you drowned during baptism."

When the grades were tallied, however, Perry Ray was at the top of his class. And within weeks, he was facing his first revival crowds, where his shortcomings were on full display.

Nary a soul, it seemed, wished to run the risk of drowning.

Perry Ray's miracle was a single column of type near the bottom of the front page. It appeared under a headline that said: "Beatle's 'Jesus' Remark Draws Fire."

The Beatle was John Lennon, of course, and his remark was this: "Christianity will go. It will vanish and shrink. I needn't argue about that; I'm right and I will be proved right. We're more popular than Jesus now. I don't know which will go first— rock 'n' roll or Christianity. Jesus was all right but his disciples were thick and ordinary."

The article noted that the remark had prompted some radio stations around the country to ban Beatles music from the airwaves. It also said that the Beatles had refused further comment on the matter, and that record stores reported sales were steady despite the furor. In all, it was a restrained account, an oversight the *Barrington Chronicle* would make up for in the coming days.

Not much of a miracle, eh? Read on, Macduff.

These days, when members of rock groups behave like circus geeks, but don't dress as well, Lennon's bit of blather would be seen for exactly what it was: the indulgent ramblings of someone who believes that being born with an ear for music qualifies him as an expert in a whole range of social issues. You see this a lot with celebrities. I suppose that's the result when tens of thousands of strangers gather to watch you do your job, then cheer wildly when you're done. I wonder what I'd be like if after I finished sweeping the floor of the bus station every night, a stadium full of people applauded and women threw their panties at me. I'd probably be just as insufferable.

Besides that, Lennon was proved dead wrong. Within

twenty years, he was in the ground, the Beatles were only a memory, and a resurgent Christian population had nearly hijacked the Republican party—not that I'd have missed it much, mind you.

But at the time, Lennon's comments were blasphemy. What was to become the sixties was already taking root, and citizens of places like Barrington were convinced their children were being led to drugs, promiscuity, and Godlessness. They were, of course, and most couldn't get there fast enough. Had anyone sought to entice me into such a life, I would have tossed my broom aside in a second and started looking for the love beads. But I was already closing in on forty then, and an aging deaf-mute who lived in a bus station storeroom wasn't exactly what the youth revolutionaries had in mind as they sought converts.

They also didn't have a recruit in Perry Ray, who was more of the thick and ordinary kind.

He took the newspaper back to Maddie Tynan's kitchen and sat at the table. Were he telling this tale, he doubtless would describe the moment as one that brought a feeling of being bathed in a hot light, or filled with a heavenly joy, or some other tommyrot that the faithful usually trot out just before performing a bit of nastiness in the Lord's name. But he's not narrating this. I am.

The bonfire was surely born at that moment.

For the week he preached the Barrington Baptist Church revival, Perry Ray stayed with Mrs. Maddie Tynan, the widow of prominent attorney Alford Tynan, mother to Tolliver and Tallasee Tynan, and one of the most talkative old hens who ever roamed the earth.

The housing of the revival preacher with Mrs. Tynan was a relatively new tradition, born in Tolliver's ascension to the

pulpit of Barrington Baptist. During most of the history between the church and Barrington Baptist College, the student
chosen to preach the summer revival had been lodged at the
home of a family selected by a complicated formula involving
desire, piety, current standing with the preacher, and level of
weekly contribution to the collection plate. But when Tolliver
became God's head coach at Barrington Baptist, he began
bunking the rookies with his mother—mostly because it meant
someone else had to listen to her talk for a week, I suspect.

"I believe we'll just have a cold supper this evening if that's
all right with you," Maddie said when Perry Ray returned to
the kitchen with the newspaper. "It's too hot to cook. I've really
got to do something with this kitchen. I need new wallpaper
and I don't know how long this old refrigerator will last. I
bought that refrigerator in 1948, Tallasee was just a little thing
then, now here she is graduated from college and already gone
from home. I told her she needn't be in such a rush to leave, it
wouldn't hurt a young woman to stay at home until she gets
married. I lived at home until the day Mr. Tynan and I got married, it was the proper thing to do then. . . ."

Trying to follow Maddie's stream-of-consciousness conversations was a full-time job, so most people in Barrington
had learned to nod occasionally and throw in a phrase like, "Is
that right?" during a pause, but otherwise go about their business. I was the only person in town Maddie didn't talk to, for
the obvious reason, but the only one in town who actually listened to her. I filled in many a blank by keeping an ear cocked
toward the old gal.

Perry Ray, being new in town and naturally deferential to
boot, didn't interrupt. He nibbled at the breakfast Maddie had
set out and waited for his chance. When she stopped to take a
swallow of coffee, he said, "When does Tolliver get to the
church in the morning?"

It was a newcomer's mistake. Asking Maddie a question

put her into overdrive. It was an hour before Perry Ray arrived at the church, and he almost missed Tolliver altogether.

They met in the door of the church office, and Tolliver's irritation at being delayed was apparent. As it turned out, he was on his way out to gloat with his co-conspirator over their looting of the church's insurance fund. And he hated being interrupted.

*It's a peculiar thing about Protestants that they'll move easily be-*tween denominations. Social and professional standing as much as the nuance of belief often determines which church a Protestant will attend. A junior bank officer may be a lifelong Methodist, for instance, but you can bet that if the senior executives are all Baptists, he'll undergo a conversion as dramatic as that experienced by Paul on the road to Damascus. All faiths probably see this. I'm sure that somewhere in the Orient, a Buddhist is considering switching to another temple because he just found out the local rice merchant attends there, even if it means twisting his topknot to the right instead of the left.

Over the years, Barrington Baptist Church achieved a critical mass of social standing, and by 1966, it was the church of choice among Barrington's influential citizens. However large it loomed above the city, it dominated the mental landscape even more. How that happened involves a short lesson, so sit up straight and look lively.

The great thing about history is that the more time that's involved, the easier it is to boil events down to a few phrases. I can summarize the first two thousand years of the Christian church this way: An entrenched, corrupt ruling class (the Romans) persecuted a despised minority (the Christians) by killing them, enslaving them, or feeding them to their pets (the lions). But the Christians had a purity of purpose while the Romans had gout and vomitoriums. So the Christians eventually triumphed, and wasted no time in establishing their own entrenched and occasionally corrupt aristocracy (the pope, his cardinals, et al.) and persecuting another despised minority (the Jews). Once a few minor bits of housekeeping were out of the way (the Crusades, Inquisition, Salem witch trials, etc.), Christians finally were able to settle down to the task of dictating social behavior (ordering the subservience of women, emphasizing the importance of filling the collection plate, and humiliating anyone caught touching their tingly parts).

But because so much of this tale focuses on Tolliver, it's worth taking a closer look at matters of church and state—the Baptist church and the state of Georgia, particularly.

Despite its current position at the top of the church heap, the Baptists actually were late to the party. Aside from the Anglicans, who were the official God franchisees among the upper-crust British settlers, the Presbyterians had the early foothold in Georgia. They established the coastal town of Darien in 1736, then began moving into the Georgia backcountry. But they were handicapped by the quaint notion that their ministers should actually know something, and the time they spent educating their preachers limited the speed of their expansion. So the Presbyterians were soon eclipsed by the Baptists and Methodists, who placed little value on educating their ministers.

By 1800, the Baptists and Methodists were the big two, and if you weren't one of them, your application to join the Frontier Country Club and Indian-Killing Society was likely to be returned with a firm "No thanks."

But in the course of the next fifty years, two things happened. One was the split in the Baptist and Methodist churches over the issue of slavery. In 1845, after a Georgia slaveholder was refused a seat as a denominational missionary at some national Baptist blowout, the Southern Baptist Church was founded. Soon after, the Methodists followed suit, meaning that the state's two largest churches had irrevocably lined up on the Simon Legree side of the slavery debate. This added to the siege mentality that had already developed in this insular Southern society.

The second thing that happened was the Great Revival. Beginning at around the turn of the nineteenth century, the revival was one of those periodic efforts to spread God's message far and wide. Preachers fanned out into the hills and hollows of Appalachia, setting up temporary camps to which an area's farm families would come to be baptized or spiritually replenished or have the devil driven from them. Those meetings, usually held in warm-weather months, continue to this day at many Southern churches as the summer revival.

Curiously, though, the Great Revival also highlighted the differences between those rural congregations and the city churches. As the towns grew, their churches became refined. Where a mountain-dweller thought nothing of rolling on the ground and speaking gibberish as he banished the devil from his soul, his lowland planter counterpart preferred to sit in a pew, cushioned if possible, and be scolded on his shortcomings in a civilized tone. And as those differences became apparent, the schisms developed. The Separates and the Primitives evolved out of the Baptists, for instance, while the Methodists saw the Holiness and, later, the Pentecostal churches hived off. In each case, the new church voiced the same complaint that had been at the core of the original Protestant movement: that the established church had created a clerical aristocracy that claimed exclusive access to God.

So by the time Tolliver Tynan heard the call, the South

was producing two species of minister. One was a presentable, cultured sort who had a comfortable life and a privileged spot in the social strata; the other was a polyester-wearing yokel whose idea of theological discourse was a debate over whether one passes the snake to the right or left.

Tolliver, of course, evolved into one of those urbane princes of the church. It's just as well. A less refined congregation, being more familiar with serpents, might have wondered how one found its way to the pulpit.

He was a handsome and stylish fellow who managed the clever trick of combining moral superiority with a touch of obsequiousness. When Tolliver thundered at the faithful that they were coming up short in the sacrifice department—that Jesus had given his very life!—no one took it personally, for each parishioner was confident that Tolliver was addressing someone else. It was his key to a successful career: scold publicly, fawn privately.

And fawn he did. Many times, while working around the church, I heard Tolliver tell a member of his flock—usually a well-to-do one—how much of an inspiration he was.

"I've often wanted to tell you," Tolliver would say to the fawnee of the moment, "that there are times when I have doubts about myself and the future of this church. But when I think of your leadership and contribution, I'm filled with strength. This congregation is built on a few people like you, and I want you to know that I understand that."

Delivered in a low, intimate tone and always as part of a chance encounter, it was very effective. How could it not be? Here was the head of Barrington's largest church confessing that in times of personal crisis, your very existence helped him cope.

Tolliver was clever about other things, too. He used the church's kitchen—which sat idle most of the time—to open a downtown lunchroom, making sure any parishioner who worked nearby felt obligated to eat there regularly. He set up a schedule of volunteers to staff the nursery during the week, with the understanding that mothers who wanted to shop could drop off their kids at no charge. He arranged business-men's prayer breakfasts and made clear that God approved of profit, the more the better.

In short, Tolliver made the church a private club with a privileged membership. A few social climbers might hop aboard from time to time—some chicken-killing trailer trash with an ambitious wife, for instance—but otherwise Barring-ton Baptist was an exclusive train with a vigilant conductor.

Which made it all the more bothersome to have a loser like Perry Ray Pruitt underfoot that week.

I'd bet that when Perry Ray looked in the mirror, he wanted to see Tolliver: husky-shouldered, lots of prematurely gray hair, and fine white teeth that had never had a wad of tobacco rested against them; dark blue suit and white shirt as his vestments, with shoes that were always polished; a jaunty, confident man-ner, and a voice with the pitch and resonance of the lower keys on the church organ. Tolliver was what young preachers wanted to grow up to be.

Perry Ray was what young preachers feared they really were: a gangly bumpkin whose mishandling of the summer re-vival probably would have destined him to a lifetime of labor in Africa for the Christian Ladies' Relief Mission.

Christians are great ones for ruminating on the devil and the temptations he throws in the path of the virtuous. But in reality, all tragedies are born of human weakness. The devil just isn't involved, except perhaps to pick off a few pieces, hyena-like, as things happen. The devil didn't make Tolliver a vain, deceitful, and corrupt man, and he didn't make Perry Ray a fall guy. But for a brief moment in history, there was room for mischief when Tolliver's greed collided with Perry Ray's panic, and in that collision the devil did indeed have his way. In hindsight, it's clear who did his bidding. I was sure justice was being served when I set out to snare Tolliver, but I'm not sure anymore. Tolliver deserved what he got, Perry Ray didn't deserve what he got, and I've spent twenty-five years wondering whether I really had any business working offstage pulling levers, turning on spotlights, and tripping the trapdoor.

7

Shortly after Perry Ray Pruitt escaped Maddie Tynan's kitchen and intercepted Tolliver at the church, Tad Beckman of the *Barrington Chronicle* and I also showed up there, both hoping to get a bit of Tolliver's time. Perry Ray was already huddled inside the office, but Beckman knew he would be next. My place at the bottom of the pecking order was a given. So he went down the hall to chat with the church secretary, no doubt hoping to eavesdrop on a phone call and peek at a letter or two. We shared the same instincts, Beckman and I. The only difference was that the things I learned from nosing around I kept to myself, which made me a snoop. Beckman shared the things he learned with thousands of people, which made him a journalist.

I sat on the floor outside Tolliver's office door, waiting to be paid for the wash-and-wax I'd just completed on his car. Making me wait was another of the small indignities Tolliver had imposed upon me for years. But I was used to them by then, and besides, docility was an important part of my persona. When I'd had a bellyful of Tolliver or others like him, I usually found a quiet way to even things up. For instance, that whole egg I'd dropped into Tolliver's gas tank just a few minutes before would dissolve within days, gumming up his fuel line and leaving him stranded along the road. I hoped it would be raining. And dark.

So I sat patiently and listened as Perry Ray explained his idea for a revival-rescuing bonfire.

"I saw a story in the paper this morning," he began. "Did you see it? About the Beatles?"

Tolliver didn't say anything. I imagined he was just shaking his head, giving Perry Ray a damn-your-eyes look and waiting for him to go on. I wasn't the only one Tolliver tried to discomfit. Anyone below him on the social ladder was vulnerable, and Perry Ray—the inept son of a street preacher—was especially so.

Still, Perry Ray gamely pressed on. "One of the Beatles, it was John Lennon I think, told somebody that he was more important than Jesus Christ. He said he was the new Christ and that the rest of the Beatles were his disciples."

I heard Tolliver shift in his seat, his attention apparently piqued. "Who did he say this to?"

"I don't know exactly. Some newspaper person, I guess. But don't you just know it's true? That hair, and the way they shake it around while they play that music. Making girls scream and faint and everything. You bet he thinks he's Jesus. An evil Jesus who wants to take advantage of those girls and make them . . . do things."

There's something that could keep a psychoanalyst busy for a year: sex, Jesus, young girls, rock 'n' roll, and hair, all simmering together in the soup of Perry Ray's mind. God only knows what his dreams were like.

"What's that got to do with us?" Tolliver asked.

"We can't just let him get away with this, can we?" Perry

Ray cried. "There has to be a response. Decent people have to stand up to this blasphemy. What are young people supposed to think when they read this and church leaders like you and me stay quiet?"

Tolliver's voice got cool. I knew he would be annoyed by Perry Ray's assumption that there was an equivalency of leadership between them. "Perhaps you should worry about leading people to the front of the church," he said, referring to Perry Ray's goose egg on the baptism scoreboard.

I could tell from Perry Ray's voice that Tolliver had drawn blood. "I know it's not going so great. But I think this is a chance to generate some interest in the revival and send a message to heathens at the same time."

"What exactly are you suggesting we do?" Tolliver asked.

"Let's have a bonfire! We'll announce to everyone that they should bring their Beatle records, maybe even all their rock 'n' roll records, and throw them in. We would be drawing a line. We'd be saying, 'This is enough,' to people like John Lennon who dare to blaspheme the Lord."

Beware of the preacher in the full grip of his fury. Had John Lennon walked into Tolliver's office just then, Perry Ray would have been upon him like a Doberman on a civil rights demonstrator. But it wasn't John Lennon who came in at that moment—it was Tad Beckman, ensuring that what was just a bad idea instead would become history.

"Mr. Tynan, do you mind if I interrupt? I've got another appoint-ment soon and I just wanted to ask a quick question," Beckman said.

"Come in, Tad," Tolliver said. "Have you met our revival preacher, Perry Ray Pruitt?"

"Pleased to meet you, Mr. Pruitt," Beckman said. He was polite, for a Yankee.

"Hello, Tad," Perry Ray replied, sounding a bit peeved.

"What did you want to ask?" Tolliver said.

"Did you see the article in the paper this morning? About John Lennon?" Beckman said.

Thus, I sat outside the door of a preacher's office and heard the birth of one of the great misadventures of our time.

Beckman wanted a cheap story. If you're a careful reader of your local daily paper, you see them regularly. A reporter selects three people at random, solicits their opinions on a hot topic of the day, then writes one of those finger-on-the-pulse-of-the-public articles that editors love because it makes them feel that they're really tuned into the community without having to actually leave the office. In this case, however, Beckman was exercising some initiative. Rather than waving down people who happened to wander by his table at the local diner, he was out collecting comment from local ministers. He'd already gotten expressions of outrage from the Methodists and Presbyterians, and was on his way to the Pentecostals.

But it still was destined to be a thumbsucker of a story with a predictable headline: "Area Ministers Shocked by Lennon's 'Jesus' Comment." That is, until Tolliver weighed in.

He was remarkable. Only moments before, he was prepared to dismiss Perry Ray's idea. But with Beckman there, pencil poised above notepad ready to memorialize his every word, Tolliver made the bonfire his own—complete with date, time, and rationale.

"Words aren't enough," he told Beckman. "I can't articulate the depth of my disgust. I fear for our children and I'm disappointed in our adults. Decent Christians must respond to this, and respond in clear and forceful terms."

"Respond how?" Beckman asked.

"We won't argue with Mr. Lennon. I don't find it productive to argue with fools. We will instead send a message that's both philosophic and economic. We want to hurt Mr. Lennon in both his heart and his pocketbook.

"On Sunday evening, in the parking lot outside Barrington Baptist Church, we will light a fire. It will be a beacon to Christian people of all persuasions, a light to help them beat back the encircling darkness of Godlessness. The people will be asked to bring their Beatle records, and all the other records, books, and magazines that have become our society's repositories of sin, and hurl them into the fire.

"Perhaps it shall be here in Barrington that the cleansing fire of righteousness is lit and spread across the earth."

I have to hand it to Tolliver—he could turn a phrase. Beckman didn't say anything for a long time, the quiet interrupted only by the scratching of his pencil as he wrote down Tolliver's words. He got them all, too. His article the next day had all of Tolliver's little speech, with the Methodists and Presbyterians relegated to the last few paragraphs and the Pentecostals ignored altogether—either because Beckman never got around to them, or he neglected to take a translator who could speak in tongues.

And he did a good job. Despite his being a Northerner, a Jew, and a general irritant to waitresses all over town—who had to listen to him whine about the lack of real food like bagels, and what exactly is a grit anyway?—Beckman's article captured the situation deftly. He had a bit of history of Barrington Baptist Church and its social importance, a couple of paragraphs about Tolliver, a compact summary of Lennon's comments, some background on the Beatles, and finally, a few sure-fire read-me phrases about grim determination (Tolliver), the young preacher-apprentice (Perry Ray), and plans being hatched as the village deaf-mute sits uncomprehendingly outside the office, oblivious to the controversy swirling around him. (Me. I hope you're reading this, Beckman.)

Actually, two articles were prepared. One version, stripped of the stuff most local people already knew, ran in the *Barrington Chronicle* the next day. An expanded version was sent to the Associated Press's Atlanta bureau, where an editor put it out on the national wire that evening.

By Saturday morning, Tolliver was on the front page of the *New York Times*. By Saturday afternoon, the CBS television news crew was settling in at the Georgian Hotel in downtown Barrington.

After Beckman and Perry Ray left Tolliver's office, I went inside. I think he'd forgotten I was still waiting.

"Did you clean out the inside?" he demanded loudly. Like everyone else, Tolliver understood I could read lips, but also like everyone else, he tended to raise his voice, subconsciously compensating for my supposed deafness. "I'm not paying for a half-assed job. You got the seats and the floor mats, too, right?"

I nodded, waiting for our little ritual over payment to begin. "How much do I owe you?" Tolliver asked, knowing full well what he'd already offered.

On the small pad I always carry, I wrote: "$100."

As he reached into his back pocket for his wallet, he turned his head to the side. "When hell freezes over, you dummy," he muttered, then handed me five dollars.

8 When Tolliver was done stealing Perry
Ray's idea for the bonfire, he walked to the offices of the Percy
Queen Insurance Agency to review his plundering of Barrington Baptist's insurance fund. It was, for Tolliver, a promising
morning.

Despite Percy's testimony at the trial, I'm here to tell you
he and Tolliver were in cahoots all along. They had an opportunity to make a bit of quick money: Tolliver had an investment tip of clearly criminal origin, but no money to act on it.
Meanwhile, Percy Queen was sitting on a pile of money—the
church's insurance fund. Both were devoid of conscience—
which is why they would have gotten away with it had it not
been for the bonfire—and neither of them had a sense of ac-
countability, which is why the trial was such great entertain-
ment as each blamed the other: Percy declaring that Tolliver
never told him how he learned of the highway plans, and Tolliver declaiming that he was just a poor country preacher who
depended on Percy to tell him what was right and wrong in
business deals.

The whole affair had its roots in a conversation I over-heard six months before Perry Ray's revival week. I was work-ing at the church, painting the floor molding in the corridor outside Tolliver's office. Tolliver and a man I'd never seen be-fore had gone inside and shut the door, but an open transom window allowed me to hear their talk. From the initial ex-change of pleasantries, it was clear the man hadn't polished a pew very often.

"We don't see nearly enough of you," Tolliver said. "How's your lovely wife . . . uh, Sally?"

"Betty," the man said. "She's fine. Mr. Tynan—"

Tolliver interrupted him. "Unless you're here to talk to me about back taxes, call me Tolliver." This was a vintage Tol-liver expression, and I knew it was accompanied by a look of friendly concern that said, "Tell me what troubles you, my friend, and if it involves your neighbor's wife don't skimp on the details."

"It's not about taxes, but I did want some advice," the man said. "Something's come up at work and I feel myself tempted to do a wrong thing. I guess I'm just here for a little moral sup-port."

"Why don't you tell me about it," Tolliver said.

I could hear the man shift around in his chair. "Ah, well, I don't know exactly how to explain this. When I say some-thing's come up at work, what I mean is where I used to work. Until a few weeks ago, I had a job with the state highway de-partment, but I've been fired. I'm a drinker, Tolliver, and it's cost me my job and my wife, who's not really fine, by the way. Or maybe she is. I don't know. The point is, I haven't seen her in months. She used to drink with me, but some time back she found Jesus again and stopped. Then she started in on me, and there wasn't a moment's peace in my house until she left. She attends a Holiness church now over near Bate's Branch. She al-

ways thought Barrington Baptist was a little too highfalutin."
Realizing how that last bit sounded, he added, "She just never
felt comfortable here. Her folks were from way up in the hills."

I knew Tolliver couldn't have cared less if some drunken
hillbilly woman decided to trade the company of community
leaders and social icons for a bunch of backwoods, snake-han-
dling gospel shouters. But he still managed to sound hurt as
he expressed magnanimity. "The choice of a church is a personal thing. If her spiritual needs are being met, then it's not
for me to second-guess her decision. As for your problem, I'm
afraid my advice is going to sound familiar: You simply have to
control your drinking."

The man sounded puzzled. "I'm not here to talk about my
drinking. In fact, I've stopped. It runs in streaks with me, you
see, and right now I'm as sober as a judge."

It was Tolliver's turn to sound puzzled. "Then what exactly is it I can help you with?"

"Well, I don't know how to explain it, so I'll just say it. I
stole something from work before I left, and I need to return it.
But I'm afraid that if they know I took it, they'll prosecute me,
so I need someone to return it for me, without letting them
know who it's from. So I thought I'd ask if you might do that
for me."

"I think you'd better tell me a bit more," Tolliver said.

There was silence for a moment, as if the man was mulling
how much to reveal. Then he blew a deep breath through his
lips and said, "OK, but this is just between us, right? The highway department is touchy about this stuff. What is it that
Catholics do when they talk to the priest and admit to doing
wrong stuff, but the priest never talks?"

"Confession," Tolliver said.

"Yeah, confession. This has to be like confession. I want to
set things right, but I'd prefer not to have some state investiga-

tor ask me about it later. There was a scandal over this very sort of thing a few years back, a whole bunch of people got fired and one or two even stood trial. It got a lot of coverage in the Atlanta papers."

"This will be just between us," Tolliver said.

"All right, here's what happened. I knew I was probably going to get fired a few months ago when I stopped getting assignments—"

"What exactly did you do?" Tolliver asked.

"Oh. I suppose I should have mentioned that. I did title searches. When the highway department is doing the initial planning for a new road, I had to track down the owners of the land involved. When it comes to actually buying the land, an independent title company steps in, but for the early work, it's all done in-house.

"But like I said, I stopped getting assignments a few months back. Of course, I was missing work a lot. I'd fallen off the wagon pretty hard that time, and when I came in at all, I came in late and left early. I can see now that I got what I deserved, but at the time I was resentful about it. I knew what was coming and I had a typical drinker's attitude about it. It wasn't my fault and I was being singled out for punishment. So I decided to take my retirement plan with me.

"You know the interstate highway that now dead-ends over near Suwanee? It's going to be extended to Greenville, South Carolina, in the next few years. The people who own land along its route are going to get rich. The state wants to avoid condemnation proceedings every step of the way, so it's paying top dollar for the land. It's all federal money anyway. And if you happen to own land in a spot where an interchange is planned, you've got money in the bank. In other places where the interstate's been completed for a while, some of those interchanges have become little cities, with gas stations, restaurants, motels, stores, everything. So I figured that because there's money to be made, and because the department had seen fit to fire me and leave me without my benefits, I might as well get in on the bonanza."

I heard the sound of a fat wad of papers being dropped on a desk.

"This, Tolliver, is the proposed route for I-85, complete with legal descriptions of the properties involved in Soque County. That road is going to swing by no more than three miles from where we're sitting, with a major interchange planned for the spot where U.S. 441 crosses Snell's Mill Road. I was planning to use this to make some money, either by buying some of the land or by selling the information to a developer. But I've decided it ain't worth going to prison for. So I need you to return this without saying how you came to have it."

"Why haven't you just thrown it away?" Tolliver asked. "I'll be glad to return it, of course, but the removal of temptation is what's important, and you've already taken that step."

"I was going to burn it with the trash one day, but it didn't have the right feel to it. The department will never know it's missing. It's from my own private files at work, and when I left they were all dumped in a box and sealed up. No one will go through them. So how can I truly be rid of a sin if no one knows the sin was committed? I guess I thought it was important for someone to know."

What happened after that is best told by Percy Queen. I can't claim to have overheard any of the talks between Percy and Tolliver, but Percy was only too happy to describe them in detail when the prosecuting attorney began tossing off words like "fraud" and "grand theft." It was a sensational trial—literally every reporter who came for the bonfire just five months before returned to see Tolliver in the dock for defrauding his own church—and Percy was a star witness. Because I can't improve on his testimony, I'll let the trial transcript tell the tale.

PROSECUTOR: Mr. Queen, will you please tell us how you know Tolliver Tynan.

PERCY: My company, the Percy Queen Insurance Agency, writes the policies for Barrington Baptist Church.

PROSECUTOR: How long have you known Mr. Tynan?

PERCY: We grew up together. We covered three counties in that old car of his, chasing girls and looking for liquor. Then he became a preacher and gave them up. Or at least he says so. [Laughter.]

Part of Tolliver's considerable charm was his history of being a rogue in his younger days. There's something appealing about men of God who admit to once having been on a first-name basis with sin, and Tolliver struck the right note with it: he never talked about it, but any reference was met with a rueful grin and a shake of his head. As the years passed, the stories became more benign and until the trial, people had forgotten what a thoroughly miserable son of a bitch he really was. But I remember.

PROSECUTOR: As the person who handled insurance matters for Barrington Baptist Church, you probably had many talks with Mr. Tynan about money matters, is that right?

PERCY: That's right.

PROSECUTOR: Mr. Queen, would you tell the court how Barrington Baptist Church's insurance matters are handled.

PERCY: Well, as you might imagine, the church has a number of policies. It has coverage against all the normal disasters like floods, tornadoes, and fires. It also has liability coverage, in case somebody falls down, then sues the church because the floor was too slippery. There's also coverage on Tolliver's car and house, and the church pays for a life insurance policy on him. I wrote all those policies, but I'm an independent agent, so there's not just one insurance company involved. The church gets its insurance from several different companies.

PROSECUTOR: How are you compensated for your work?

PERCY: I collect commissions from the companies that provide the insurance.

PROSECUTOR: How does the church pay for the policies? Are the insurance companies paid directly?

PERCY: No sir. The church basically keeps its insurance money in a bank account controlled by my agency. It's common with big clients for me to keep separate accounts for them at Barrington Bank and Trust. When policy payments come due, my agency writes checks from those accounts to pay for them.

PROSECUTOR: Does the church keep a balance in this account, or does it send the money over when it's needed?

PERCY: Both, sort of. We know when policies come due, of course, and we generally have an idea how much is needed to cover them. But because there's so many, and because they come due at various points over the year, it's more efficient for the church to deposit money in the account every month.

PROSECUTOR: So money will occasionally build up in the account.

PERCY: Yes sir. There's one stretch every year when we go several months between policy renewals. It tends to pile up then.

PROSECUTOR: And when is that?

PERCY: Late winter, early spring.

PROSECUTOR: Did Mr. Tynan ever make any unusual requests of you regarding insurance matters?

PERCY: Well, he drove off the road once while hurrying to get to a deacon's meeting and wanted to know if he could waive the deductible by calling it an act of God. [Laughter.]

PROSECUTOR: Aside from that. Specifically, did Mr. Tynan come see you in February 1966 to discuss the church's insurance?

PERCY: Yeah, although it started off as a talk about a business deal.

PROSECUTOR: Did he explain what the business deal was?

PERCY: Not at first. It was all what if—you know, what if someone had an investment opportunity, a chance to make serious money, but didn't have much to put into it. So I explained about OPM.

PROSECUTOR: And what's OPM?

PERCY: Other people's money. I told him that in the business world, smart people never risk their own money. They use somebody else's. Shareholder money, bank money, pension fund money, whatever.

Prosecutor: Did Mr. Tynan ever reveal the business deal?

PERCY: Yeah, he finally came around to it.

PROSECUTOR: What did he say?

PERCY: He said he'd found out which route the new interstate highway would take near here. And he said if someone were to buy land at a certain spot where an interchange was planned, that someone would probably make a whole pile of money.

PROSECUTOR: Did Mr. Tynan say how he'd gotten this information?

PERCY: Nope.

PROSECUTOR: Did he tell you where this interchange would be built?

PERCY: Nope. What he said was, Percy, I've got the highway plans and you've got the OPM. He proposed that we throw in together and buy the land.

PROSECUTOR: And what did you say?

PERCY: I told him it wasn't against my religious be-

PROSECUTOR:	liefs to make money, but I'd prefer to have something more than faith to go on.

PROSECUTOR: So you had misgivings about the whole scheme?

PERCY: You bet I did, especially when he started talking about where he would find the money to pitch in for his end.

PROSECUTOR: Where did Mr. Tynan say he would get the money?

PERCY: He said he would just borrow it from the church's insurance fund.

Setting aside Percy's more self-serving bits of the tale, his testimony made clear that the two of them cooked up a plan to use the insurance money to buy the land, then use the land as collateral on a loan to reimburse the fund before the next round of policy payments came due. According to Percy, they didn't expect much trouble buying the property; it was a remote patch of crossroads land that had long ago been taken out of farming and left to scrub pines. They expected it was theirs for the asking, and afterwards they'd only have to wait for road construction to begin and the commercial interests to come sniffing around. It was all very tidy. You can see how Tolliver and Percy came to believe it would work.

The only thing they didn't count on was another buyer.

You may wonder, by the way, how this trial occurred without involving the man who gave Tolliver the highway plans. The answer was to be found in an issue of the Barrington Chronicle *published a couple of months before the trial. In it was a short item about the death of one Stanley Markham, a former highway

85

department employee killed in a one-car accident that the sheriff declared was alcohol-related.

Only four people knew of the connection between the unlucky Stanley Markham and Tolliver Tynan: one was Stanley himself, and he was dead; one was Tolliver, but he was on trial and unlikely to bring it up; and one was me, and I hadn't said a word in more than twenty-five years.

The fourth was the fellow named Archibald Thacker, and as an elderly black man with secrets of his own, he kept quiet.

9

It's a peculiarity of literature that few people have written about the South without having the black folks in those tales teeter between two stereotypes: the cartoons that populate some stories, like Margaret Mitchell's Mammy, or the dignity-in-the-face-of-oppression types who serve as moral counterpoints, like Mark Twain's Jim or William Faulkner's Dilsey. To find real-life black folks—people who manage to be angry, proud, ambitious, conniving, intelligent, malcontented, and insular, all at once—you have to go, well, to real life.

Meet the Thackers.

The Thackers used to be everywhere in Barrington. When I set the garbage out behind the station twice a week, a Thacker drove the truck that picked it up. When Tolliver finished with his flock every Sunday, a Thacker was there to straighten up the church. When I was called to rake someone's lawn, a Thacker was there standing on a ladder with a paintbrush in hand. When any sort of menial, dirty service was needed, a Thacker provided it.

Archibald Thacker oversaw things from a home on the wooded edge of Buttermilk Bottom. A widower, Arch had six sons, each of whom married and raised a bunch of kids of his own, meaning there were dozens of Thackers in Barrington. One whole edge of the Bottom was populated exclusively by Thackers, and it was a mess: old appliances littered the yards, cars stripped of their tires sat on concrete blocks, yards were choked with weeds, and packs of hounds trotted anemically behind any passerby, their eyes hopeful and tongues lolling.

On any given day, you would find at least a couple of the Thacker men sitting on their front porches—almost all of which needed a few new boards—killing time while their children played in the dust. Or you'd see several of them gathered in a yard, blowing mouth harps and sawing away on fiddles, the very picture of idleness that many Southern white folks still take to be genetically coded. Even their names caused white people to shake their heads in wonderment. In order of their ages, Archibald's sons were George Washington Thacker, Abraham Lincoln Thacker, Thomas Jefferson Thacker, Matthew Mark Thacker, Luke John Thacker, and Marcus Garvey Thacker.

If all this seems a little too perfectly stereotyped, there's a reason why. Archibald Thacker, who now occupies a spot on the *Forbes* Four Hundred list of wealthy Americans, knew that white people wouldn't bother him as long as the Thackers were happy, no-account niggers.

(Before you get all hot and bothered about my use of the word "nigger," let me say a couple of things. It's an ugly word, and I don't use it casually. And I won't stretch my eyes innocently and proclaim that it can't be all that bad, considering that black folks use it among themselves all the time; that's a typical white person's dodge. But the fact of the matter is that Archibald used that exact phrase in an interview with *Forbes* in

1983. "We could never have succeeded in those early days if people had known we owned all the businesses they dealt with," he said. "As long as we were happy, no-account niggers working for white people, things were fine.")

The Thackers were all employed by two companies, Soque Waste Haulers Inc. and Barrington Building Services Inc. As far as anyone in town knew, both firms were owned by Are Em Jones, who made a career out of being white, dumb, and lucky.

I remember Are Em from school. He was a few years older, which was a shame, for had we been the same age, he would have been a much more inviting target for Tolliver. He was big and goofy, and memorable only for his endless nattering about what he was going to do to the Japs as soon as he got old enough to enlist. He did indeed eventually sign up, and how he survived the war is a mystery; he saw combat, albeit in Europe rather than the Pacific, and went ashore during the Normandy invasion. He was the sort of soldier the winning side generally has the most of: obedient, malleable, and expendable. As Ulysses S. Grant proved in places like Cold Harbor, having a few thousand Are Em Joneses in your arsenal to absorb bullets is a decided advantage. But no bullet ever found Are Em, and he returned to Barrington after the war with a chestful of campaign medals and a new name.

The name came as a result of the Army's inability to come to grips with the notion that Are Em's full and complete name was R. M. Jones. Reportedly, his parents couldn't agree on a name when he was born, and he was given initials instead. After having countless army documents returned to him because he'd failed to use his full name, R.M. finally wrote "Are Em" on one form. That document sailed through the army bureaucracy without a hitch, and he was then known, officially and forever, as Are Em Jones.

Had it not been for the war, Are Em surely would have been a chicken killer or a rock chopper. But combat veterans, even dim-witted ones, usually believe they deserve something more rewarding than a spot on the processing line at the local poultry factory. Are Em wanted a desk job. One day in early 1946, he found it in the Help Wanted pages of the *Barrington Chronicle*.

The *Forbes* article on Archibald Thacker summarized what happened. "Race, of course, was the unchanging factor behind every decision. Thacker couldn't openly operate the firm because he was a black man in a segregated Southern city. So he needed a white man as a front. But because few white men of the era would work for a black, Thacker couldn't even do the hiring himself. So a lawyer from Atlanta was dispatched to Barrington with a detailed profile of the ideal candidate: affable, presentable, local-born and -reared, with a low ambition and a high tolerance for Rotarians.

"The quaintly named Are Em Jones was the third interview of the day, and Thacker's recruiter knew within minutes he'd found his man. Jones was given the job, along with a one percent stake of the company to satisfy both appearances and corporate records. For the next thirty years, Jones was the public face of one of the most successful enterprises to come out of the postwar South. The fact that it was engineered behind the scenes by a black man made it perhaps the greatest sleight-of-hand trick in American business."

This was possible, of course, only because Are Em was dumber than dirt. And what the *Forbes* article tactfully avoided saying was that when Thacker's company went public in 1983, Are Em was humiliated. It was bad enough to have his lifelong charade exposed to the world; but to have the real owners turn out to be the very bunch of dark-skinned garbage haulers he'd employed for years was too much. Despite getting a nice severance package and cashing out his one percent share—which together netted him $3.2 million—Are Em died a bitter old man.

It's a troubling thing to learn that much about your life all at once. Take it from one who knows.

Through the rest of the 1950s and 1960s, Archibald Thacker and his family quietly went about the business of getting rich. A pattern established itself early: When any family member—in the course of hauling trash and cleaning buildings—noticed a new business opportunity, a note was made and passed to Archibald. Once a week, he called his lawyer in Atlanta with detailed instructions; and once a week, the lawyer called Are Em to tell him of some possible new contracts he should check into. Are Em would dutifully trudge off to some construction site or new home development and find a builder who was just beginning to think about things like regular garbage collection or janitorial service. When business grew to the point where the existing crews couldn't handle it, the lawyer would suggest during one of the weekly calls that Are Em consider adding a couple of men; the next day, the brother of one of Archibald's daughters-in-law would show up, asking for work. When one of the old trucks seemed to be finally resisting further efforts at repair, Are Em would find that the lawyer had anticipated the problem and already called dealerships all over north Georgia for the best deal on a replacement. Are Em developed a reputation in Barrington as a canny businessman, and he was just dopey enough to believe he deserved it.

Archibald made sure the Thackers had a reputation too. Like everyone else, I took the family at face value: they were just a few more of the many beaten-down black folks that populate the South. But one afternoon a couple of years before the bonfire, I overheard a conversation that made me believe otherwise.

91

George and Abraham, Archibald's two eldest sons, had pulled their truck into the alley behind the station to collect trash. Normally, I had everything out back waiting for them, but that day I was late. So as I stacked the week's refuse for them, they perched on the truck's bumper and took a cigarette break.

"Daddy was pretty hot last night," Abraham said.

"Yeah, he gets like that sometimes. That man doesn't ever let up, does he?" George said.

"I didn't think a nigger could turn that red. When Rachel told him she was going to give that baby an African name, I thought he was going to explode."

"I got called away for dinner, so I never heard what happened. She and Daddy get into it?" George asked.

"She tried to stand up to him. She said, 'I'm a grown woman and a college graduate and I can make my own decisions.' But he just rolled right over her. He told her she knew what she was getting into when she married Marcus. He said he wasn't going to have everything ruined by a damfool woman. You should have seen him. Stomping around the yard, waving his arms and hollering about pride."

"I've heard that before. What's that saying he uses?"

Abraham grinned. "He said it, all right. 'Cheap displays of pride.'"

"How many times in your life did you get the pride lecture?"

"Man, I couldn't even put on a clean shirt without hearing from him about it. Set out for a little trim on a Saturday night and he's talking some stuff as you're going out the door. Drive me crazy."

"Rachel's getting a taste now," George said.

"Yeah. And he used some Latin on her too. Her eyes got big and I thought she'd drop that baby right there. She's so used to seeing us haul garbage, she forgot we're all college graduates."

"Marcus got himself a handful."

"You hear about her cleaning the yard?" Abraham asked.

"I saw Daddy bringing stuff back from the dump the other day. Was that for her?"

"Uh-huh. Yard looked nice, too, all raked and everything. He just stopped the truck and kicked all this stuff off."

"Tires, I'll bet," George said.

"Bunch of stuff. Tires, an old washing machine, a busted-up chair. He just pushed it off the back of the truck and told her to tell Marcus to get this stuff set out right."

"What'd she do?"

"Nothing," Abraham said. "She just stood there, hands round the bottom of that big ol' belly, looking like she wanted to cry. After he drove off, I went across the road and said, 'Listen, girlfriend, you got to get with it. You got to remember the reason we do this.' She said OK, but I can see it's tough on her."

"Sure it is. She had an easy life up in Philadelphia, her daddy a doctor and all. Marcus tells her his daddy owns a business in Georgia, she thinks it's going to be like home."

"That's right. Then she gets here and finds out she's got to live in Uncle Tom's cabin."

"I figure she was carrying when they arrived," George said. "She's been so mad, I know Marcus ain't been close to her since then."

I had finished stacking the trash and was standing in the doorway, out of sight of the truck.

"Looks like ol' Sammy's got this stuff ready," George said. I heard them both stand as a cigarette butt went skittering across the alley. "You ever hear what Daddy says about him?"

"No, what?"

"He says Sammy reminds him of those house niggers from the slave days. He don't say nothing, he don't miss nothing."

◆ ◆ ◆

I've spent a lot of time working side by side with black folks—after all, I'm the only white handyman in town—and I'm no stranger to Buttermilk Bottom. But the fact that it took the conversational equivalent of the Rosetta stone to open my eyes was testimony to the curious blindness white people have to the affairs of their black neighbors. I was no different. While I prided myself on not missing a thing that went on in this town, a whole business empire had been created right under my nose. And its creator had accurately reduced my essence to a single pithy observation. The watcher had been watched.

There was much to be deduced from that conversation. It was clear Archibald owned the business that employed his family. And it was clear that the Thackers were all much better-educated than anyone suspected. Most interesting, though, was learning how hard the family worked at disguising its success from white folks. If Archibald was importing junk from the dump to decorate yards and prohibiting African names for his grandchildren, then it was likely that everything else in his corner of the Bottom—from the broken-down look of the homes to the impromptu blues sessions on the porches—was a similarly orchestrated sham. The scope of deceit was impressive; if you conclude that the presidential/biblical/historical names Archibald gave his sons were part of the plan—names that fit exactly the white Southern belief of quaint Negro practice—then this effort was decades in the making.

It worked. These days, Archibald is near the top of every list of America's most successful black entrepreneurs. But I'm not here to just repeat a success story that's already familiar to readers of the financial press. I'm here to fill out the record, and there are two significant chapters left out of the Thacker saga.

Both figure directly in what happened at the bonfire that August and in its aftermath.

It's said that behind every great fortune is a great crime. That's not true in Archibald's case, however. His crime was routine and ordinary.

Archibald ran moonshine. He didn't manufacture it and he didn't sell it. He was strictly a transport agent, a teamster with a specialty. In the late 1950s, he saw an opportunity to enter the field, and with his typical business acumen he soon came to dominate it. Within ten years, the industry was essentially dead and Archibald's career as an outlaw was over. But as best I can tell, those ten years provided the capital for Archibald's empire building. Before that, he was a modest success, making a living and providing jobs for his family. After that, he was a tycoon. You draw your own conclusions. I certainly have.

One bit of evidence of Archibald's success as a runner is that there is no mention of the Thackers in the U.S. Treasury Department records of the era. State records likewise virtually overlook them. One surveillance report I found in a file mentions "a colored in a garbage truck seen talking to subject"; and during the interrogation of a moonshiner in north Georgia, the suspect told agents that he'd given all his whiskey to "two niggers in a garbage truck" whose names he didn't know and whom he paid in cash up front to deliver it. The transcript shows that the agents clearly didn't believe it. Indeed, the thought that this Snuffy Smith character from the Jim Crow South would turn over his corn whiskey to a pair of black strangers was beyond belief—unless you'd seen what I saw behind Barrington Baptist Church the day of the bonfire.

I don't know exactly how the Thackers came to be liquor runners, but I can make a good guess. Before I do, though, I need to explain a bit about the white liquor industry.

I'll start with the name: It's called white liquor because moonshine is clear when it comes out of the still, as opposed to

95

the bottle-and-bond legal whiskeys called red liquor. Soque County was one of those places where moonshining flourished, thanks to a combination of several circumstances. It was a dry county, which didn't mean there were fewer drinkers, only that its drinkers had to turn to illicit sources. Its residents were largely of Irish and Scottish descent, and carried a strong distilling gene through the generations. Its hilly, rocky soil didn't lend itself to large-scale cultivation, meaning there were many small-farm owners looking for any financial edge. It was heavily forested with numerous small streams, which as you'll see is a key need for moonshiners. And there was just enough leftover Confederate sentiment to make antimoonshining efforts seem like yet another example of Yankee federal oppression.

Despite all that, it's always been a mystery to me how anyone who knows even a little bit about how moonshine is made can drink it.

The broad outline is simple: mash—a mixture of cornmeal and water—is fermented, and then cooked until it condenses and a distillate is extracted. The whole process can take as few as five days, and typically produces over a hundred gallons of high-octane liquor. No special materials are needed; indeed, your local car junkyard could yield much of the stuff you need to get under way. Problem is, that's exactly where many moonshiners begin.

Take the job of fermenting mash, for instance. A moonshiner usually doesn't wish to wait for the natural process of fermentation, so he seeks to help it along. One common way is to perch chickens on the edge of the mash box, in hopes they'll add some nice organic matter to the mixture when they do their business. More businesslike moonshiners, however, don't wait for chickens' bowels; they'll simply lower a burlap sack of manure into the mash, or toss in a dead possum. But disgusting as this is, it beats what eventually came to be the preferred method: a car battery dropped to the bottom of the mash box.

The car junkyard also provides radiators, another key piece of equipment. Once the mash is fermented and the whole mess begins cooking, a moonshiner often uses a car radiator as his condenser. A particularly scrupulous man may have bothered to flush it first; otherwise, drinkers are rewarded with a dash of antifreeze and lead salt in their refreshments.

On top of all that, the whole lovely process usually takes place in the woods, open to nature and all its bounty. There are two reasons for this. Moonshiners need both access to firewood and cover from government agents, and a deep-woods location provides both. Also, the spent mash has a distinctive smell, so the still has to be well away from other people—ideally, there's a stream nearby to carry off by-products and waste.

Finally, after our happy hillbilly is through slopping around in the woods to get his hundred gallons of homemade, he'll add rubbing alcohol or paint thinner to boost the proof, guaranteeing the headache of your life, if not something more memorable—like blindness.

Once all this is done and the revenooers dodged, the moonshiner faces a second challenge: getting his product to market. In legend, the transportation of moonshine was done by young men in fast cars. In fact, it was an equal-opportunity business. Distribution was the moonshiner's Achilles' heel, and virtually anyone with a vehicle willing to risk being caught with a hundred gallons of untaxed liquor could make money. This is where the Thackers came in.

Of course, you don't just show up at the still and announce, "Hello! I know we haven't met, but I'm a friendly Negro in a garbage truck who's here to deliver your moonshine. Cash up front, please." My guess is that Archibald was recruited by someone who realized that garbage haulers, by the

very nature of their jobs, are everywhere; their movement between the countryside—where the county maintains its landfill—and all points of the city is not only not suspicious, it is
expected. Exactly who gave the Thackers their first transport
job has been lost to history. But by the early 1960s, the Thacker
family apparently monopolized the business in Soque County.
As I said, I'm doing a large bit of guesswork on this, but it's
based on two facts.

First, there's this excerpt from a police report of a 1961
traffic accident between a car and a Soque Waste Haulers
truck: "Truck sustained damage to driver's side door and front
quarter-panel. Also, what appeared to be an auxiliary gas tank
was knocked loose from frame onto road."

Second, here's what the head of the Atlanta office of the
federal Bureau of Alcohol, Tobacco, and Firearms had to say in
his 1965 annual report: "Still seizures under Operation Dry Up
increased 22 percent during the year and interdictions during
transport were up 13 percent. While the trend in the region is
clearly positive, there appears to be an isolated development
worth keeping an eye on. In one part of the north Georgia sector, there appears to be a movement toward bulk transportation. There have been notably fewer interdictions in the area
in recent years, but local demand has remained steady. One in-
formant told agent [name deleted] that distillate is now usually
gathered in single holding tanks, rather than in individual con-
tainers, prior to transportation. If this apparent move away
from 'jars and jugs' is seen in other areas, the agency may want
to consider an adjustment in its Tactical Response strategy."

But two facts don't prove a theory. An eyewitness account
does.

I'd been hired by Tolliver to stack the wood for the bonfire. He'd
arranged for the owner of Barrington Lumber to drop off a

load of scraps and mill ends. With it came a solid tree trunk, about eight feet long and sawed flat on both ends. In the middle of the church parking lot, I tipped the log on end, then laid the board scraps against it, tepee-style, but with lots of room between them. Underneath the boards were the piles of dry brush and twigs I had scrounged earlier that day. All it needed was just a splash of gasoline around the base to get it started. As I stood back and admired my work, I wondered if there weren't some bonfire-building genes in me; as the torch was laid at Joan of Arc's feet, I suspect that some guy who looked like me was hoping that the fire flared up nice and terrible, lest the inquisitors turn their attention to him.

I'd stepped inside a janitor's closet in the church to wash up, when I heard an engine. When I looked out the window, I saw it was a garbage truck, with Archibald and one of his sons in the cab. It was midafternoon, and the church was deserted. The truck pulled up close to the building, stopping at a door at the back of the church, directly across from the steps that led up to the baptismal font.

"Go in and get it drained," Archibald said. "We ain't got all day."

Fascinated, I watched as Archibald and his son Matthew pumped a hundred gallons of high-proof moonshine into the baptismal font. It flowed through an ordinary garden hose that snaked out from under the truck, up the steps and into the font; I could hear the low buzz of the electric pump that pushed the moonshine along. I guessed that the liquor was carried in a tank bolted to the truck's frame, and that the pump—presumably driven by the truck's generator—expedited its off-loading. It was a superb smuggler's setup.

I could guess how it worked. Moonshiners probably knew to call the company and, under the guise of arranging garbage collection, let the Thackers know where the liquor was supposed to be picked up; another call for collection the same day would tell them where it was to be delivered. Payments would be made directly to the company or, if the moonshiners dealt only with cash, turned in as payment for some bit of piecework hauling.

And at the center of this would have been the hapless Are Em Jones, unknowingly coordinating a large-scale smuggling and money-laundering operation. Do the math and you'll understand why people thought he was a sharp businessman: the average still could produce as much as 120 gallons of white liquor and a reliable runner could demand $2 a gallon for delivery; assuming that over the course of time the Thackers came to dominate the market and were making at least one delivery a day, Are Em found himself with up to $100,000 a year more than the company's garbage operations should have reasonably produced. As business grew, Archibald's lawyer from Atlanta would call Are Em to tell him to buy another truck, another tank and pump would be quietly retrofitted, another Thacker in-law would be hired, another chunk of Soque County would fall to the growing Soque Waste Haulers monopoly, and another Treasury agent would scratch his head and wonder who was transporting all the liquor.

By my rough accounting, Archibald's smuggling operation probably generated at least $1 million for his company and, when it ended, left him with a debt-free powerhouse that dominated the hauling industry in the state. But on this sultry August afternoon, our budding tycoon was most concerned with getting the font filled with liquor and his aging butt out of sight before someone wandered in.

"You get it drained?" he asked when Matthew came out through the door. The two of them were just below the window of the closet where I stood.

"It's just about done," Matthew said. "I never realized how big that thing is. Tolliver must like to dunk 'em deep."

"Run the hose up the steps and let me know when the water's gone. We ain't got much time."

I heard Matthew drag the hose to the lip of the font. After a moment, he said, "OK, Pappy, let her rip."

"Did you close the drain?" Archibald asked. "Or are we gonna just dump this down the sewer?"

"Damn. Hang on." After another moment, Matthew said, "Hit the pump. We're ready."

The electric motor began humming and I could hear the soft gurgle of liquor being pumped from the tank. Archibald and Matthew stood in the shade of the church and waited.

"Do we deliver anything for that cracker again?" Matthew asked.

"I don't know. Probably. It wasn't his fault. He's got a new mash run started and he needed to get those jugs emptied."

"Yeah, but we ain't a storage facility. What are we supposed to do when people give us stuff in the middle of the day and tell us to keep it till midnight? We got other deliveries to make."

"We'll see how this works," Archibald said.

"What if someone decides to get baptized tonight?"

"It won't happen. Everybody's gonna be outside tonight. Besides, I hear that boy they got preaching this week couldn't get a tadpole near water."

"How are we going to get this stuff back into the tank?"

"We'll unhook the hose from the truck and leave it here with one end in the font. If we make sure there's liquid in the hose, it'll siphon right back in. We'll jam a rag into the other end and tape it up tight."

"You mean it will drain itself back up that hose?" Matthew asked.

"Jesus, don't you know anything about hydrodynamics? What'd I send you to college for anyway?"

"I was a philosophy major, Pappy. Luke studied science."

Archibald gave a snort and the two of them stood quietly. The motor hummed for a while, then stuttered and turned itself off.

"We're done. Let's get out of here," Archibald said.

As I listened to the truck drive away, I realized I really should get to know my new business partner a bit better.

10

CBS News broadcast its first report from Barrington on Sunday, a couple of hours before the bonfire. Its camera crew, producer, and reporter had spent Saturday getting "visuals," as the producer called the bits of landscape they filmed, and putting local people in front of the camera to chat about the Beatles.

Thanks to the efforts of one Iris Saperstein—an archivist at CBS News who received a letter from Samuel Ayers, Ph.D., asking her assistance in the preparation of a scholarly examination of the conflict between religious conservatives and popular culture—here is a transcript of the news report from Barrington on August 7, 1966. I can't show you the film, of course, but if you've seen any television news feature, you can imagine it: lots of shots of the courthouse, the church, the Confederate monument, the colorful natives engaged in uniquely Southern behavior like eating grits and scratching coon hounds behind the ears, Tolliver earnestly decrying the decay of society, close-ups of racks of Beatles records, a random man-in-the-street reaction, and a big finish focused on

103

the stacking of scrap wood that was to become the bonfire later that day. That's me doing the stacking, by the way.

Voice-over: "August is typically the hottest month in Barrington, Georgia. It's a time to sit on the front porch, drink iced tea, and discuss the prospects of the University of Georgia Bulldogs in the coming college football season. It's hotter than ever in Barrington this August, but it doesn't have anything to do with the weather. Many of the thirty thousand residents of this picturesque city north of Atlanta will gather tonight around a bonfire to express their feelings about the Beatles, John Lennon, and rock 'n' roll in general."

Unidentified teenage girl: "I'm throwing all my Beatles records in that fire tonight. They can melt down into hair spray, for all I care."

Voice-over: "The people of Barrington are outraged by John Lennon's recent observation that the Beatles are more popular than Jesus Christ. In places like New York City, that claim was hardly more than a momentary diversion. But here in the Bible Belt, where portraits of Jesus are found in many homes and signs along the road remind us that Jesus saves, John Lennon's comments were a call to arms."

Tolliver Tynan: "We're engaged in a battle with a subtle and clever enemy. Jesus taught us that the face of temptation is often disguised. For too long, we've believed that rock 'n' roll was harmless, and now we see that it's not. Thanks to John Lennon, it has shown its true face."

Voice-over: "That was Tolliver Tynan, head of Barrington Baptist Church, where later tonight a bonfire will be held. The citizens of Barrington are being encouraged to bring their rock 'n' roll records and throw them into the fire. And church leaders are not stopping there. They say they will ask radio stations to stop playing rock 'n' roll, record stores to stop selling rock 'n' roll, and auditoriums to stop hosting rock 'n' roll performances."

Tolliver Tynan: "Let this be the start of a new age of decency."

Voice-over: "Chances are, there will be a big crowd here tonight. Barrington Baptist is the largest church in town. And it's also the time of the summer revival here, a week-long event during which members renew their faith with prayer meetings every evening. There's the feeling here that this protest is part of a larger effort. There have been protests in other Southern cities and some radio stations have said that for now, the Beatles are off their play lists. It's not certain that the protest will last. Some people, like record store owners, think the whole thing will eventually blow over. But then again, folks said the same thing about rock 'n' roll itself ten years ago. From Barrington, Georgia, this is Neal McNeal reporting."

Curiously, CBS didn't use its best interview with a Barrington resident. It was with a woman the camera crew intercepted as she exited a downtown store. I overheard the whole exchange.

"Hi, I'm Neal McNeal with CBS News. Can we ask you a few questions?"

"Why?" the woman asked.

"Well, this is for a news report we're doing on the bonfire," he said.

"So you'd like to film me while you ask questions."

"Yes, that's right."

"Isn't that something you should tell people right up front?" she said.

McNeal's reply was huffy. "I thought it was obvious. Perhaps you noticed the man behind me with the camera."

"If I showed up naked for a date, would you assume you'd hit the jackpot?"

"It would seem a safe assumption," McNeal said. He seemed confused at the quick shift of the conversation.

"But you wouldn't know until you asked," she said.

"I did ask," he said.

"You asked if you could ask questions. You didn't ask if you could film."

Behind him, McNeal's cameraman and soundman were smirking, enjoying his discomfort. Although he probably preferred to just walk away, it would have looked like a retreat, so McNeal forged on. "All right, I'll try again. Can we ask you a few questions and film your response for possible broadcast to hundreds of thousands of homes across America?" He said it as snottily as possible.

"Sure," the woman said, smiling innocently.

"What did you think about John Lennon's comment that the Beatles were more popular than Christ?"

"He's probably right."

"He is?" McNeal said.

"Sure. Only a few people took Jesus seriously in the beginning, and when he started drawing crowds, the religious establishment had him killed. The Beatles draw more people to one concert in New York than probably saw Jesus in his whole life."

"But wasn't Lennon being blasphemous?"

"Only if you assume he was talking about Jesus. If you take it as a comment on the state of modern culture, it's not blasphemous at all. Has anyone considered that he was trying to point out the absurdity of a society that pays greater attention to a singing group than to Jesus?"

"Perhaps," McNeal said. "But maybe it's exactly what it seems: a rock 'n' roller who's so successful he thinks he's become a god."

"Oh, don't be so self-righteous," the woman said. "He's a creature of mass communication. If reporters didn't hang on his every word, none of this would be an issue."

McNeal clearly didn't like where this was going. "OK,

that's enough," he said to the cameraman, then turned back to the woman. "Thanks for your time. I'm not sure how much of it we'll use, but I appreciate it anyway." Then, wanting the last word, he added: "By the way. If you're in the habit of showing up naked for dates, perhaps we can get together."

"I don't know," the woman said. "It might be a waste of my time. Seeing you with that microphone makes me think you like having long, stiff objects near your mouth." She sauntered off as the cameraman and soundman howled in laughter.

McNeal never asked the woman her name. As a result, the irony of the whole scene escaped everyone but me: the news crew had just gotten a pro–John Lennon point of view from the minister's own sister, Tallasee Tynan.

Barrington, like most Southern cities of the day, was idle on Sunday afternoons. And on the day of the bonfire, the torpor was even more pronounced. The humidity and a sense of expectancy hung equally heavy in the air. Dogs lolled under trees, porch swings and rockers creaked quietly, and countless pitchers of tea were brewed, cooled, and consumed. A few radios were tuned to the Atlanta Braves, who only that year had moved from Milwaukee, but otherwise there were few sounds. It was almost as if the lesser beasts, under the same instinct that tells them when tornadoes are imminent, had taken cover while the more evolved creatures indulged in their madness. What else would you call it? A possibly sociopathic and certainly corrupt preacher, aided by an inept sycophant, was about to re-create some medieval ritual of banishing demons with fire, while professional voyeurs recorded the event for posterity.

An apologist for Christian zealotry might claim that however barbaric it is to fuel hysteria and destroy all nonconforming thought, at least a virgin wasn't sacrificed in Barrington that night. Well, that apologist would be wrong. One was.

11

How Archibald and I became partners is a story that begins in a brothel. I bring it up partly to explain the second untold chapter of the Thacker saga, but also because I know there's one question that eventually crosses everyone's mind: How does a deaf-mute who lives in a bus station broom closet get laid?

The short answer is this: Once a month, he takes the bus to Athens; he walks up the hill from the station to the county courthouse, then takes a left; he follows the street for a mile or so until it slips underneath two railroad trestles; then he takes the second right and goes to the back door of the middle of the three homes nestled against the river; he is welcomed inside, chatted up for a few moments, then ushered into a private room where he presents his courting tackle for the obligatory disease check, negotiates the terms of his pleasure, and proceeds to dance the dirty hula. In terms of its regularity, rituals, and making of a donation, it's a bit like going to church, except you know your prayers will be answered.

I visited the first time when I was nineteen. I got directions by listening while a college boy waiting for a bus instructed a buddy on how to find the brothel. A couple of days later, I joined Jenkins at Lucille's lunch counter and handed him a note. It said: "I believe I'll visit Athens this weekend."

Jenkins read it and passed it to Lucille without comment. She read it, looked at me sharply, and said, "Why?"

I shrugged. I had been in Barrington for almost ten years, was fully grown, and had never left the county since the morning I woke up alone on the bus. This was my rebellion, I suppose; I didn't have to explain anything to anyone.

"Maybe you'll decide to enroll in college," she said. Lucille was still smarting that I had dropped out of high school against her advice.

I shrugged again and Jenkins gave me a bemused look. "Have a good time," he said. "Just don't fall in love with somebody else's bus station."

That Saturday afternoon, after hurrying through my usual chores, I put on clean clothes, doused my head with hair lotion, and boarded the bus to Athens. Three stops and ninety minutes later, I was standing in front of the station, getting my bearings and sniffing the wind.

The depot was down the hill from what seemed to be the center of town, so I started walking up toward a traffic light. Sure enough, after going about a half-mile I found myself on a busy corner, with the arched entrance to the university on my right and the courthouse spire poking up among the trees two blocks away on my left. It was a lively corner, with stores open to the sidewalk, students streaming across the street from the campus, and farm families crammed into pickup trucks circling the block. I dawdled awhile in front of a newsstand, reading newspaper headlines and magazine covers before finally setting out for my destination. I knew when the last bus left for Barrington, but I wasn't sure I wanted to be on it. The day would seem like less of an adventure if it merely ended with me on a bus; I wanted to enjoy the feeling of not knowing what was going to happen next. I wasn't even sure I knew where I was going. So far, the directions I'd overheard were true, with all the landmarks in the proper place. But suppose I knocked on the designated back door and some mill worker's tired wife answered? Or what would happen if I found the brothel, but discovered there was some secret word I was supposed to know to get admitted? Would I be left in the yard, alone and frustrated, while voluptuous beauties taunted me by pressing their bare breasts against the windows, making clear exactly what was being denied me for lack of a word? Or, worst of all, would I be allowed in to then be made fun of? Perhaps that was how whores entertained themselves: they waited for a skinny, badly educated, emotionally scarred kid who lived in a bus station and pretended he was deaf to show up for his first dipping of the wick, then humiliated him.

As it turned out, I needn't have worried. I tramped by the courthouse, down the hill past the second trestle, then turned onto the second street. Sure enough, there were three houses there with the river visible behind them; I stood for a long minute facing them, then walked around the back of the middle house and knocked on the door.

It was opened immediately by a woman, who pushed the screen aside and said, "C'mon in, honey. I thought sure you were just gonna walk off again."

I stepped into a low-ceilinged sitting room that years before someone had tried to make into a Victorian parlor. But the chairs and sofa had seen too much use, the curtains were a bit tattered, and the whole place was suffused with the smell of tobacco and sweat. My hostess herself showed some signs of weathering. Her face was lined and she was missing an eyetooth, which gave her a lopsided look when she smiled. But she was a friendly sort, and although she wasn't exactly dressed for Jesus, she was turned out nicely enough and could have walked to the store without drawing a second look. That's more than I could say for the other three women in the room.

They weren't naked, but they were as close as you could get to it and still have something on. One was reading a magazine, another was sitting idly with her leg thrown over the arm of the chair, while the third was working her nails with a file. I wish I could tell you that the air was charged with eroticism, and describe the resident staffers with phrases like "heaving bosoms lifted in welcome" or "creamy white thighs that parted to reveal a glimpse of Venus' treasure." But the fact of the matter was, they looked pretty ordinary. All three regarded me with a dispassionate curiosity for a second or two, then resumed their business. I heard the door shut behind me.

"Afternoons are a little slow for us," the madam said. "So take your time. Talk to the girls and decide who you like."

I turned to look at her, then tapped my ear with my finger. She looked at me blankly, then it registered. "You're deaf?" she said.

I nodded. The three women looked at me again, this time with more interest. For a long moment, no one moved or said anything. Finally, the woman with the magazine said, "Hey, deaf people have money too. I'll take him."

She set the magazine aside and waggled her fingers, my invitation to help her stand. I took her hand and pulled her up, and let myself be led down a corridor to a bedroom. We went in and she shut the door.

"Let's take a look at you," she said. She gave the front of my britches a tug, then stepped back and waited.

She hadn't been the prettiest of the three—that would have been the one with the nail file—but there was something good-humored and earthy about her that made me relax. She

111

was around thirty and well fleshed through her bosom and hips. She had kicked off the high-heeled slippers she'd been wearing when I first came in, and I noticed her feet were wide and flat. Walking behind her in the corridor a few moments before, I'd noticed how the shoes gave her hips a provocative roll when she moved; but as she walked around the bedroom without them, her farm girl feet somehow made everything feel domestic and unthreatening.

I didn't know then that an inspection of my privates for signs of venereal disease was part of the routine, so I was unsure what I was supposed to do. I unbuttoned my top button and pulled my shirttail out, but then waited. Even though the window was shaded, the overhead light was on and I felt self-conscious. I didn't have much practice at waving my wand while women watched.

We stood looking at each other for a moment. Then she took the bottom of my shirttail, pulled me over to the bed, and, while sitting on its edge, worked my britches and underwear down around my ankles. She pushed my shirttail up and motioned for me to hold it there.

"We'll just take a quick look at you," she said again. With her head ducked down, she pulled my foreskin back, felt under my testicles, and ran the tips of her fingers along the skin underneath the hair. I had my stomach sucked in and was chewing on my lower lip; deep in my gut, I could feel an all-hands-on-deck, this-is-no-drill scramble. When her touch stopped being clinical and started getting to the business at hand, I was afraid my guys were going to blast the big gun before I'd even gotten my feet disentangled from my clothes.

But I was in the care of a professional who knew that commerce precedes pleasure. When she had me pointing to high noon, she stopped and gestured to a chair next to the bed. I waddled over and finished undressing. She continued to sit on the edge of the bed, and when I glanced up at her, she asked, "Can you understand me?"

I nodded. "For three dollars, we can do this once," she said. "But if you've got five dollars, you can stay an hour."

I gave her ten dollars. I had a lot backed up.

Her name was Judy. For the next year or so, I traveled to Athens faithfully once a month for an hour's therapy. (I'd discovered in our first session that the effort-versus-return ratio in the second hour got all out of whack; what I could do twice in the first sixty minutes I was barely able to do a third time in the next sixty. I think Judy was a little miffed when, on my second visit, I scaled back to an hour. The ratio was precisely reversed for her: she had worn me out early during my first visit, and coasted through the session's second hour. But commerce cuts both ways, don't you know.) However, when I arrived one Saturday for my regular game of hide-the-weenie, I was intercepted by the madam.

"Judy's gone," she said. "But I have another girl who would like to meet you."

Thus I became an inheritance. When this new companion moved on some six months later, I was passed on to yet another. After that first visit, I was never again faced with making a choice; my patronage was a commodity to be divided among the women by some mysterious process, in which I had no role other than to show up. That suited me fine. Aside from a residual affection for Judy—'tis indeed a hard-hearted man who doesn't think kindly of his first bed partner—I had no emotional attachment to any of them. I knew exactly my value to them: I observed a regular schedule, paid well, and didn't ask stupid questions about how they came to be whores. In return, my mate of the moment was ready when I arrived, gave me an

113

honest hour's effort, and never once sent me to the doctor with the clap. They were scrupulously clean and always inspected my dangler. If other businesses were run as satisfactorily, most lawyers would have to make an honest living.

I made my visits for eleven years, until the day I found a body in the whorehouse.

It was 1960 and I was visiting on a Sunday, which was unusual for me. It tended to be a busy day for the handyman sector of the economy, and I was riding this bull market through my peak earning years. (Translation: I had discovered that having money beat the hell out of not having money, so I took on so many jobs that they spilled over into the Sabbath.) As a result, my monthly visits to Athens generally were made on Tuesdays, when the bus schedules were such that I could get there, conduct my business, and return by early afternoon. But on that Sunday, my job box at the station was empty, and I was bored, so on an impulse I went for a belly-bump.

I was greeted at the door by the madam. Over the course of the years, she had been the one constant in my visits. While the working girls had changed too many times to count, she alone had been at the door every time. Curiously, she never told me her name. But she had become a nodding acquaintance, and our relationship was like the one you develop with letter carriers, waitresses, gas station attendants, or anyone else you encounter on a regular basis in a certain setting. Beyond the fact that she administered the whorehouse where I was a customer, I knew nothing about her and she knew nothing about me. Or so I thought.

"Well, this is a surprise," she said. "But I hope you're not expecting Candy. She's off with the curse."

I just shrugged. Candy was an energetic sort, but she was a

bit too backwoodsy and had a walleye to boot, meaning I could never quite figure out if she was looking at me or at something just over my shoulder. It was disconcerting. I had gotten into the habit of turning off all the lights before we started.

So the madam paired me up with a woman I'd never seen before and we made our way to one of the bedrooms. But before I'd even gotten my belt unhitched, we were interrupted by a piercing scream from the hall.

Of course, by that point I'd pretended to be deaf for so long that I ignored it reflexively. But my companion jumped to her feet, fluttered a hand near her chest for a moment, then yanked the door open to see what all the hubbub was about. I followed her out to the hall where, two rooms down, one of the other women stood in the doorway. She was nude, with her hair tangled and the shadow of a bruise already showing above one of her breasts. She was breathing hard and gathering herself to scream again, when we came into the hallway.

"He's dead," she cried. "Oh God, he's dead."

"What happened?" asked my mate.

"I don't know. His face turned purple and he started bucking and humping so hard I thought he was gonna squish me. Go in and tell me if he's dead."

The other rooms had emptied and the hall was full of naked or near-naked strumpets and their customers. We were all gathered at the entrance to the room, but no one moved to enter. The distraught whore, crying and hiccuping, was led away by one of the other women; still no one went in. Finally, the madam elbowed her way through the crowd to the doorway and said, "Well, somebody come with me to see about him." When no one stepped forward right away, she grabbed the nearest arm—which was mine—and pulled me into the bedroom.

The man was facedown on the bed, with his head turned

115

toward the wall. One arm was tucked under his stomach while the other was flung out over the edge of the mattress. He had a big, white, soft body with freckles across his shoulders, and his neck and the forearm I could see were tanned dark. The madam went to the far side of the bed and squatted down to peer into his face.

"He sure looks like he's dead," she said. She lifted the arm that hung over the bed and pushed it toward me. "Pull him over and let's take a look at him."

We managed to wrestle the man onto his back. As we did, his head lolled over and faced me. It was Jenkins.

I sat on the floor and cried. There was still a knot of people gathered in the doorway, and my reaction set them to murmuring again. The madam went to the door and asked one of the women, "Did Queenie ever get settled down?"

"Yes," the woman said. "Should I call the police or something?"

"Don't do anything. Just go back to your room."

She closed the door and sat beside me on the floor. She seemed to want to comfort me, but it wasn't something that came naturally and she didn't do it well. She took a handkerchief and started to dab the tears from my cheeks, then just wadded it in her hand. She patted my knee a couple of times and made sympathetic noises, but her hand flapped away self-consciously. Finally, she just sat silently until I wound down.

After I'd wiped my face with a corner of the bedsheet, she nudged me on the arm and said, "Look up here a second." When I raised my eyes, she said, "Can you understand me?"

I nodded.

"You knew him, didn't you?"

I nodded again.

"He asked about you once. It was years ago. He wanted to know if a deaf boy had been coming here. He described what you looked like and what days you'd been in. At first, I was suspicious of him. Was he some kin of yours?"

I hesitated for a moment, then shook my head.

"I asked him what business was it of his. He just shrugged and said he knew you and wanted to make sure you were getting treated right. He tried to act real casual about it, but I could tell he wanted to know.

"I told him, 'Mister, everyone gets treated right around here,' and he laughed in an embarrassed kind of way. He said that wasn't what he meant. He said you were a lonely boy and he was afraid you'd fall in love with somebody here and there'd be a big mess."

She didn't say anything for a while, and the only sound was the ticking of a clock on the windowsill across from the foot of the bed, placed so that its owner wouldn't have to turn her head to check how many more minutes of pleasure she had to endure. Finally, she nudged me on the arm again.

"You've got to help me with this. I know a policeman who would come take him away if I asked him to, but I'd prefer not to do that. How about if you take him?"

I stared at her. What the devil was I supposed to do with him?

She'd thought of that. "What you can do is, his car is out by the shed. When it gets dark, we can carry him out there and you can drive him back to wherever he comes from. I'll bet you know where he lives. You can drive, can't you?"

I nodded. Some years before, when I'd gotten curious about it, Jenkins had taken me in his car to the high school parking lot and let me drive around. Later, when I'd gotten a feel for it, he'd sent me on short delivery missions. I was surprised I hadn't noticed the car when I came in that afternoon.

117

"Then just drive him someplace where he would have been any other Sunday night and leave him there. It'll look like he had a heart attack in his car. No one will think anything of it."

So that's what I did. Jenkins deserved better than to be found dead in a whorehouse, which would have been the only thing Barrington remembered him for. As dark settled in, I pulled the car close to a side door, and we dragged the body down the hall and muscled it into the car. I drove to Barrington and parked the car in Jenkins's usual space in the alley behind the station, then slid him across the seat toward the steering wheel and slumped him down as if he'd fallen that way. I tried to think of what a policeman would look for, and realized I had jammed Jenkins's keys into my pocket. After unlocking the station door, I tossed the keys on the car floorboard, then went inside to my storage room and cot. I lay there for a long time, waiting for something more than a rumor of sleep.

It happened just like she said it would. A policeman making his rounds just before dawn found Jenkins in the alley and had him taken to the morgue. The autopsy showed he died of cardiac arrest some hours before the body was discovered. After the funeral, he was buried in the plot adjoining the graves of his wife and daughter, with their matching dates of death.

There's one other thing I should tell you. There was something on the table beside the bed that day in the brothel when Jenkins died. I noticed it as we were moving his body: it was a tin of smoked oysters and a long-handled teaspoon. The tin was open and half its contents were gone.

Jenkins didn't die of a heart attack. His demons finally killed him.

There's a clear line that leads from Jenkins's death to my partnership with Archibald Thacker and beyond—all the way to the church bonfire and its aftermath. That's not to say none of this would have happened if Jenkins hadn't died; it's just that I wouldn't have been positioned to see it as clearly.

That line runs through McAdoo, who came just a few days after Jenkins's death to run the bus station. If McAdoo hadn't come to Barrington, I wouldn't have sought legal help from Eldon Rubicoff, the Yankee lawyer, or formed my company called Ike Enheer & Associates. If I hadn't formed Ike Enheer & Associates, I wouldn't have become a business partner with Archibald Thacker. And if I hadn't become a business partner with Arch, then the bonfire would have been remembered only as a tragic accident, Tolliver would have continued in his conniving ways, and I would have lived out my days on life's margin, an obscure oddity so woven into the fabric of this Southern town as to be almost invisible.

If I were to hold a straight narrative, I wouldn't spend much time on McAdoo. Despite being around for ten years or so, his role in history was merely to be the bridge between me and Rubicoff; and as such, he could be reasonably dispatched after a paragraph or two. But McAdoo is the means by which I'll keep you from forming too warm an opinion of Barrington. His deep well of hatred for black people was tolerated and accommodated by the citizens of Barrington, and I can't draw a portrait of this town without acknowledging that. Racism is something that lingers in the Southern soul to this day, and we as a society can only grow when we come to grips with it.

If none of that rings right—and it shouldn't, because while it's true, I'm just not that sensitive—try this: I'm going to tell you about McAdoo because I hated him and I've got a score to settle. It's my book, and if I want to burn a few pages telling you what a racist turd he was, then I'll do it.

He arrived the day after Jenkins's funeral, sent by the company to take over. I was out before breakfast that morning on a job, and returned early enough to get a couple of eggs and the last spoonful of grits from Lucille. There was a burly guy with coarse black hair sitting at her counter when I plopped down.

As Lucille set a plate of food in front of me, the man watched carefully; the easy familiarity between us must have been apparent. "Is this him?" he asked. Lucille nodded.

I ignored them and ate my breakfast. But out of the corner of my eye I could see that the man's powder-blue shirt carried the company name over the pocket. He had a big ring of keys on his belt, cowboy boots with tricky stitching on the toes and uppers, and little crescents of dirt under each fingernail. He was sipping coffee, with the remains of his own breakfast in front of him. The next time Lucille came out of the kitchen, he set the cup down and said, "Gimme some more, willya."

As she poured, he asked, "How many years have you been here?"

"Since 1936, which makes it twenty-four years," she said.

"I can add and subtract. What's your deal here?"

"My deal?" Lucille said.

"Yeah, your deal. How much do you pay to operate in our station?"

"I pay fifty dollars a month, plus five percent of my revenue. All the equipment's mine, along with the tables, chairs, dishes, knives, forks, spoons, and any food that's fallen behind the refrigerator."

"Do you pay your own utilities? Power and water?"

Lucille shook her head.

"Ever had an increase, or is that the same deal you made with Jenkins twenty-four years ago?"

"Same deal," she said.

"What about him?" he said, jerking his head toward me. "Does he pay anything to live here?"

"He works for room and board."

He considered this for a moment, then said, "I never heard of anyone living in a bus station."

"He keeps the place looking nice. He generally sweeps a couple of times a day, and the bathrooms are cleaner than the ones in most folks' homes."

"How did he get here? I heard he just showed up one day and never left."

"Nobody knows exactly," Lucille said. "He stepped off a bus and sat down outside, but nobody came for him. He was just a kid. Jenkins let him stay in the storeroom and I fed him. We both expected someone would come get him, but they never did."

"He's deaf and dumb, huh?"

"He can't hear, but if you talk directly at him, he'll understand. He won't talk, though."

He turned and tapped me on the shoulder. "Hey, buddy," he said. I looked at him and noticed the name "McAdoo" stitched over the pocket of his shirt. "You gonna live in that storeroom forever?"

Just then, old Wilbert walked in the door. He was an elderly black man who, for as long as anyone could remember, had sold sacks of boiled peanuts from a corner near the courthouse. He also was in the habit of leaving a dozen sacks for Lucille to sell to travelers; even though he understood that she was to keep a nickel for every bag sold, she never did, and I don't think he knew the difference. He was slightly retarded and completely illiterate.

"Mornin', Miss Lucille," Wilbert said as he slid the sacks across the counter. The peanuts, damp and oily, had already started to stain the bottom of the bags. I never understood how people can eat a cold, mushy thing like that. You take a perfectly good peanut—which out of the ground doesn't have the crunchy taste of a roasted nut, but a chewy, subtle flavor—and you boil it in the shell until it's a pulpy, clammy mess. Jesus, no wonder Yankees can't take us seriously. I can't figure that one out myself.

Here's something else I can't figure out: why the very presence of a Negro makes some Southern people crazy. McAdoo drew himself off the stool and faced Wilbert. "Don't you ever come in here again, you hear me?" he said menacingly. "I don't know what it was like before, but here's what it's like now: Niggers wait outside. You got it?"

"Now wait a minute," Lucille said. "I do business with him."

"Then do your business at the back door," McAdoo said.

Wilbert clearly didn't understand what was going on. His eyes swiveled between the two of them for a moment before he reached out and tried to give McAdoo a sack of peanuts. "For you, sir. On the house."

McAdoo backhanded the sack, spilling peanuts all over the floor. Without saying a word, he grabbed old Wilbert by the shirt collar and dragged him outside, giving him a rude push through the door. He then marched over to the ticket counter, reached behind it for a paper and a baggage marker, and wrote "WHITE ONLY" in large letters. Grabbing a roll of masking tape, he went outside and taped the sign to the wall next to the door. When he came back in, he headed for the lunch counter; Lucille had barely moved.

"I'm sorry about Jenkins," he said to her. "But he should never have allowed this foolishness to go on. I'll have to set things right here."

He started toward the ticket counter, then stopped and faced me. "Sweep up this mess, willya," he said, gesturing to the peanuts on the floor. "You see why you can't let niggers in?"

◆ ◆ ◆

McAdoo could keep Negroes out, but he didn't know what the devil to do about me. My presence defied his peculiar sense of order. He knew exactly where he stood in the social structure: Negroes were well below him, Lucille was just below him, the bank teller who handled the deposit of his daily receipts was below him but the loan officer was above him, Tolliver was just above him (until he learned that old Maddie Tynan was a rich woman, which moved Tolliver well above him), the owners of neighboring businesses were above him and their employees below him, and bus passengers were below him unless they wore overalls, which put them well below him. The fact that I lived in the back room of a bus station and swept the floor put me down there with overall-wearing Negroes, but my financial independence and the unique circumstance of my arrival in Barrington confused him. So he was content to treat me like hired help and refer to me as "the dummy," but he stopped short of doing what he wanted to do: get me out of the storeroom.

The man who ignores the cloud gets wet, however. McAdoo exercised discipline in his prejudices, practicing a husbandry of hate that allowed him to dispense a steady, equal measure of bile every day. Given enough time, he'd have found a way to force me out.

As I said, I did two things. First, I tried to cut his time short by sending a regular stream of letters to the bus company's headquarters, using fictive names and addresses and citing a litany of complaints about the service and facilities at the Barrington bus depot (but being careful to praise the parts of the operation I handled; for instance, several writers noted that they'd rarely seen a bus station floor as well swept and tidy). Second, I took a lesson from nature and tried to make the predator think I was too big and difficult to eat. I became a company.

It took me three afternoons in the Barrington Public Library, thumbing through the state bar directory and the Atlanta Yellow Pages, before I found what I needed: an out-of-town lawyer with a tax specialty and an ethnic name, who had graduated from a Northern institution not too many years ago, and had a solo practice or perhaps only a partner or two. In short, I wanted someone who had no ties to Barrington and wasn't likely to develop any, and I figured a Yankee Jew in a small Atlanta firm was my best bet.

Come out here and take a bow, Eldon Rubicoff.

I wrote a letter to him explaining that I needed help with a business incorporation. His reply, sent to a post office box I'd just leased, said that while he was bewildered why someone from Barrington had to come all the way to Atlanta for a simple incorporation, his mother's heart would swell with pride to know that her son's fame had spread that far, so come visit, already. Within a week, I was in Rubicoff's office, writing out answers to his questions, and a few weeks after that, Ike Enheer & Associates was born in a paper-signing ceremony. When it was done, Rubicoff leaned back in his chair, looked at me, and asked his secretary: "So, Sophie, we've had some time to think about it. What is our quiet friend not telling us?"

"I think he's a murderer," Sophie said, collecting coffee cups from the desktop. Then to me, she said sweetly, "Would you like some more coffee, Mr. Killer?"

"A murderer, he's not," Rubicoff said. "A man with a secret he is. The question is whether we should know this secret or if we're better off not knowing."

"So who should know other people's secrets? Do you go around telling your secrets, Mr. Make-a-Face-When-Your-Mother-Calls?" Sophie said.

Rubicoff shrugged and took on a haughty tone. "This man is my client and I am his trusted adviser. I'm obligated to

poke around in his personal affairs and private life. It's my job."
He took a sheet of paper, scribbled on it, and passed it over to
me. It said: "Is there anything else you need help with?"

There was. When I first got wind of McAdoo's desire to
run me out of the station, I realized I didn't have a weapon except a community's moral outrage at the mistreatment of a
quirky, deaf-mute handyman who didn't show up for work
when he thought the wage was too low. In other words, I was
defenseless. I'd had some vague notion that if a company were
involved—a firm that could suggest, in a letter to McAdoo on
my behalf, that my residency was part of some formal arrangement and describe the deal with phrases like "previous agreement" and "agreed-upon terms"—I could somehow scare him
into backing off. But in the weeks it had taken me to form Ike
Enheer & Associates, I'd concluded that this was a high-risk,
one-shot approach: If McAdoo didn't cave in right away and
instead wrote back asking to see this agreement, I was sunk. If I
concocted a contract, he surely would send it along to headquarters, where in quick time it would be exposed as a fraud.
What I needed, then, was something that would make McAdoo
think I was untouchable.

I made a scribbling motion on my palm and Rubicoff
handed me several sheets of paper and a pen. In ten minutes, I
sketched out my life in writing, explaining how I'd arrived at
the bus station, how I grew up there, and how disturbing it was
to face the prospect of eviction. I laid the poor-orphan-boy
stuff on thick, but I stopped short of revealing that I
hadn't always been a deaf-mute; like Sophie said, you don't tell
all your secrets.

Rubicoff took the sheets back and read them. He regarded
me quizzically, then started over and read the whole thing
again. When he finished the second time, he set the papers on
his desk and bellowed, "Sophie!"

She came in from the front of the two-room office. "I need you to look up some cases on oral contracts. We can take a break from perverting justice for a while. We've got a good deed to do."

As it turned out, I didn't need the law on my side, just Rubicoff.

Within a couple of days, I got a letter from him saying that, upon reflection, he had decided it was misguided to make my residency in the station a legal issue. There was a better way to handle it, he wrote, and if I didn't mind making the trip to Atlanta again, he'd explain it to me, and besides, Sophie thought I looked a little thin and overworked, so if I came she could make sure I rested a bit and ate something. So I soon found myself again in Rubicoff's office, munching on my first-ever bagel with cream cheese and nodding as he asked if I was sure that I could understand him when he talked, it's amazing how well I could read lips, you'd hardly think I was deaf at all.

"So, here's what we do," he finally said. "We give this go-niff McAdoo an award."

I stopped chewing and cocked an eyebrow.

"Look, maybe we could make a legal argument on the basis that almost twenty years of residency constitutes an implied contract, considering the fact that you've essentially worked for the bus line as a janitor that whole time and being allowed to live there was your only compensation. But even if we establish that you're an employee, the company can't be compelled to provide living quarters for you. You don't have an inherent right to occupy someone else's property. You only have a right to be compensated for your labor, and although the form of that compensation has always been a place to live, the company probably has the right to change those terms. And probably will, if we make it an issue.

"So we don't look at this as a legal problem. We look at it as a public relations problem."

The idea was elegant. The Ike Enheer Foundation—the soon-to-be established charitable arm of that burgeoning financial powerhouse Ike Enheer & Associates—would donate money to a carefully selected charity. An announcement sent to newspapers around the state would explain that the donation had been made in the name of the bus line, and specifically on behalf of its big-hearted station managers in Barrington, McAdoo and the late Jenkins, in recognition of their quiet but long-standing commitment to the underprivileged: namely, one Sammy Ayers, a deaf-mute orphan who had been "adopted" by the bus line at a tender age and nurtured in its loving grasp to maturity. (You may now dab the tears from your eyes.) The award should be big enough to command attention, Rubicoff said, but not so big as to make reporters wonder exactly who was this mensch Ike Enheer, throwing money around like there's no tomorrow.

"So do you have a thousand dollars?" he asked.

For the second time that year—first with the whorehouse madam and now with Rubicoff—things worked exactly as they'd been dictated. Several newspapers, including the *Barrington Chronicle* and the *Atlanta Constitution*, carried articles about the award. The president of the bus line was quoted as saying he was "flattered and surprised" by the honor, and suggested that he'd monitored my progress from afar over the years, having been in touch with Jenkins—and now McAdoo—on numerous occasions to discuss what was best for me. The *Chronicle*, in a subsequent editorial, congratulated not only the bus line but the town itself for its streak of true Christian compassion "that allows a deaf-and-dumb orphan to make his home in our homes, to find a place in our lives for his life."

Over three decades later, I still want to heave on my shoes when I read it. I wake up one morning irretrievably lost and scared speechless, ignored by everyone except a spinsterish grill cook and a man who thought he'd killed his family by watching some naked slattern warm up a dish of smoked oysters. Then, when I have to spend a thousand dollars—not to mention Rubicoff's fee—to ensure that I could continue to make my home in a twelve-foot by eight-foot storeroom, I learn that in fact I owe everything I have to the long-distance care of a bus tycoon and the warm embrace of a loving citizenry. It's no small wonder that I never felt the need to climb to the top of a tall building with a scoped rifle and begin shooting.

As I said, the connections are clear in hindsight. If Jenkins hadn't died, McAdoo wouldn't have showed up; without McAdoo, I wouldn't have needed Rubicoff or established Ike Enheer & Associates; without a company to hide behind and a lawyer to suggest it, I wouldn't have thought to approach my life as a business instead of a tragedy; if I hadn't been thinking like a businessman the day I overheard the alcoholic highway department employee tell Tolliver about the plans for the interstate, I wouldn't have recognized the investment opportunity; had I not pursued that opportunity, I wouldn't have hooked up with Archibald Thacker; and if Arch and I hadn't become partners, Tolliver would have walked away scot-free.

So I suppose that in a left-handed way, I owe McAdoo a debt. But damn his eyes if he thinks he'll ever collect.

Actually, there's one vital connection I've left out.
Several weeks after Jenkins died, I found an envelope on my cot. McAdoo had been busy cleaning out Jenkins's desk,

and had evidently found the envelope buried deep in a drawer. It had my name on it, written in Jenkins's handwriting. I opened it.

Inside was the key to locker 9. There was also a note, which said simply: "Sammy, I'm sorry. I knew it all along and didn't say anything. I was afraid you would go." He'd signed it with his full name. Even in his confession, Jenkins's wounds were apparent; he used distance as I used silence, to keep all else at bay.

That night, after the station emptied and McAdoo had left, I crept out to the bank of lockers and opened number 9. Inside I found my mother's suitcase.

I took it back to the storeroom and opened it. As it turned out, I wasn't lost after all.

12

Perry Ray Pruitt didn't have any better luck with fire than he did with water. The man who couldn't get a single soul near the baptismal font also couldn't get a match to stay lit long enough to ignite the torch Tolliver planned to use to start the bonfire. You'd think getting a fire lit would be an easy thing, especially if you're willing to use a splash of gasoline and a big sulfur-tipped kitchen match. But efficiency wasn't the point that night; theatrics were, and Tolliver knew he'd be a more impressive sight waving a torch than tossing a match at a pool of gas like some hapless suburban barbecue chef.

In fact, it was apparent Tolliver had put some thought into the setting. A flatbed trailer hung with bunting had been parked adjacent to the wood I'd piled just hours before. A pair of spotlights, like the ones used at movie premieres and obtained from only God knows where, had been placed on opposite ends of the church lawn and pointed straight up to heaven, creating two icy shafts of light. A small platform had been hammered together at the edge of the street and reserved for

130

television cameramen, giving them the chance to frame Tolliver, the fire, and the church all in one shot. Across the front of the church hung a banner with a quote from the Gospel according to John: "I am the light of the world; he who follows me will not walk in darkness, but will have the light of life."

Everyone was there. The pervading sense was that this would be Barrington's defining moment, and no one wanted to miss it. The other congregations had canceled their usual Sunday evening services and businesses that normally were open had locked up early. By dusk, there were several thousand people milling around the church lawn. The teenagers were gathered near the stack of wood, holding records, fan magazines, and other bits of evidence of the rock 'n' roll demons that they were now prepared to exorcise, while the adults hung back, collected together in either comfortable social groups or knots of grim-faced zealotry. There were a few blankets scattered about with families squatted down, and a handful of stray dogs darted between them, caught up in the energy. Gospel music from scratchy records drifted out from a radio station sound truck parked at the edge of the street.

There were only two nonbelievers in attendance that evening, and we found ourselves standing together for a few moments before the Lennon bashing began.

"So even you're here, Mr. Ayers," said Tallasee Tynan, perhaps the one person in the world who called me mister without a trace of sarcasm. I nodded hello.

"You never struck me as a churchgoing man," she said. "And surely you're the one person in town immune to the devil's message of rock 'n' roll."

Tallasee had a merry, troublemaking glint in her eye, and suddenly I knew that something was going to go horribly wrong that night. It was a strange feeling; one moment I'm ready to enjoy watching Tolliver lead the whole town in this silly religious ritual for a national television audience, and the next moment there's a block of ice in my gut as I realize that in some way I can't fathom, evil is about to be done. What had seemed like a festival atmosphere suddenly became proof of an incipient collective insanity. People I'd seen every day were transformed on that church lawn. Words didn't seem to match the shapes of their mouths when they talked. Children I knew to be well-behaved were acting up, and teenage girls I knew to be modest wore clothes that clung to new breasts. When people moved, they seemed to be either hung from some puppeteer's wires, or filled with some molten substance that propelled them sinuously and provocatively. The spotlights gave faces an otherworldly brightness, then made them dark and shadowy when they turned. Everything was somehow skewed a few degrees off-center. The sense of disaster was palpable, and I seemed to be the only person who noticed.

I felt Tallasee pull at my sleeve. "Mr. Ayers? You look like somebody's walked on your grave. Are you all right?"

The glint was gone from her eye and her forehead was squinched up in concern. I nodded and pulled my arm away, more roughly than I meant to. She stared at me a long moment.

"How lucky you are, to have your silence," she finally said. "All this to you is just something to watch. The rest of us have to be in it."

The ministry isn't a profession that a man like Tolliver naturally turns to. There are a number of jobs that someone without conscience, compassion, or a moral compass could embrace: serial killer, for instance, or United States senator. But preaching's not one of them, which makes the story of how Tolliver became a man of God a textbook example of life's perversity.

People don't set out to spoil their children. No parent ever brings a newborn home and announces, "I've got a great idea! Let's never discipline this child or teach him right from wrong. Let's indulge his every whim, cave in to his every demand, and make him disrespectful of adults. Our lives will be a living hell when he's little, but at least we'll be assured of neglect and abuse when we're old."

What happens instead is that parents see a spark of charm and intelligence in a child, and want to see it grow. So they provide room, under the theory that goodness will bloom naturally. Occasionally, this works. More often, it just guarantees that you raise a charming, intelligent, conniving, selfish, and greedy little soul like Tolliver Tynan.

All the factors that helped make Tolliver a moral mutant were in place early: an imposing, powerful, and distant father; a doting mother incapable of even the mildest discipline; teachers and other authority figures who gave Tolliver a free rein because of who his daddy was; and, until the sister was born much later, no other children to act as behavorial counterpoints.

Like anyone else, I'm prone to easy psychological judgments about people, and in Tolliver's case, it's indeed easy. Alford deBouchet Tynan was a truly great man who left his son a legacy that could never be matched, much less exceeded. So the son became as corrupt as the father was great.

Southern towns are no different from any other the world over in that the business barons they breed are usually self-centered, greedy villains with limited imaginations and a death grip on every nickel. Often, your typical small-town tycoon starts with one business that puts him in touch with many people to whom credit can be extended—a food store, for instance. At some point, he'll move into lending on a small scale, then branch into the distressed end of the economy: foreclosure sales, tax certificates, estate auctions, and the like. Eventually, your shopkeeper finds himself the owner of a number of slum properties, an investor in a handful of small enterprises all over town, and—if he has bothered to keep a civilized face and cover his tracks well enough—a seat on the board of the local bank. If he's good with crowds and can speak movingly about moral decay and rising crime, he can even get elected to Congress, where he can practice greed and villainy on a national scale.

On a rare occasion, though, a town can produce someone like Alford Tynan.

Tolliver's father arrived in Barrington in 1922, fresh from the University of Georgia with a law degree in hand. He was the child of a well-to-do Athens banker and doubtless would have established a tidy law practice there in short order. But he wanted to be out of his father's shadow, so with his bride, the former Miss Maddie Booten, in tow, he moved forty miles northwest to Barrington and hung out his shingle.

Alford was a clever and industrious man, with an aptitude for numbers. He handled many routine legal matters—wills, property closings, civil lawsuits, and such—but declined criminal work, telling people he didn't have the stomach for helping a guilty man stay out of jail or, worse yet, watching an innocent man be sent away. What he did best, though, was turn around troubled businesses, which is how he made his fortune and legend.

That intersection of law and commerce suited him well. Soon after arriving in Barrington, he'd begun getting cases referred to him from First National Bank of Barrington, whose president was a friend of Alford's father. One of the first cases was the foreclosure of a local clothes merchant, a man who'd defaulted on his mortgage and exceeded his credit line. Alford prepared the lawsuit, then visited the man himself to serve the papers. Normally, lawsuits are served by a sheriff's deputy or some low-level court official; most lawyers prefer to confront their opponents only in the courtroom. But it's a measure of the man that Alford delivered the papers himself anytime he filed a suit. He once said that if someone was being handed the papers that probably meant the end of his business life, the man who filed them should be there to look him in the eye.

When Alford arrived at the clothing store, he found a mess. The display windows were empty, shelves and racks were arranged haphazardly, and balls of dust lurked in the corners. But the prices were reasonable and the labels in the clothes were from top-quality mills. There were customers in the store, although they were being ignored by the clerk, who leaned against a counter reading the newspaper.

(This is all local legend, by the way. I didn't witness any of it and the details no doubt have been embellished over the years. But this is the accepted version of the beginning of both Alford's fortune and the Corey's department store chain. For more information, look up the August 1972 issue of *American Retailer* and read the profile of Cass Corey, if you can tear yourself away from the feature piece on new advances in garment tags.)

"Are you the owner?" Alford asked the clerk.

"Nope," the man said, not looking up.

After a moment, Alford continued. "Can you tell me where he is?"

"Out," the man said.

Alford let a few more moments pass before asking: "Who the devil are you?"

That brought the man up from his paper. "I'm Corey's brother-in-law. I mind the store when he's out."

"Then mind it," Alford said. "The point is to sell clothes, which you can't do from behind a counter. Those two"—he nodded his head in the direction of a pair of women pawing through a rack—"give every indication of wanting to buy something. Why don't you sell it to them?"

At that moment, a door in the back opened and a man bustled in. When he spotted Alford, with his suit and briefcase, he walked to the counter and said, "I can guess what this is about."

"My name is Alford Tynan and I'm here on behalf of the bank."

"They don't waste any time, do they?" the man said bitterly.

Alford didn't respond directly. "Is there somewhere we can talk?" he asked.

The man led him to a small storeroom that doubled as an office. In just a few minutes, Alford had confirmed his suspicions: The business had no controls or accounting, and the man's family and the brother-in-law's family were all living out of the till. The store was in a good location and had regular customers who weren't put off by the messiness, but the effect of having family members mine the cash register for household expenses had taken its toll. The man could no longer pay his suppliers, and some days there wasn't even enough money to make change.

"I've tried telling everyone that this day would come," the man said, shrugging his shoulders helplessly.

Alford didn't serve the foreclosure papers that day. Instead, he convinced the head of the bank's loan committee to put off the foreclosure for a month, then drew up articles of incorporation for Corey's Clothes, a limited partnership. He returned to the store the next day.

"I'll give you a thousand dollars to buy new inventory. I'll also make your past-due mortgage payments and I'll teach you some basic accounting," Alford told the man. "You keep the cash register locked, put your brother-in-law on salary, and make me a twenty percent owner. We've got one month before I have to come here again in a professional capacity."

The man signed the partnership agreement on the spot. That evening, after the store closed, the whole place was swept and scrubbed. A few days later, the store name was painted in the window and display dummies were set up to face the sidewalk. The brother-in-law was banished from the front counter, given the title of floor manager to soothe his feelings, and ordered to spend his day helping customers select clothes. Within a month, the store was generating enough revenue to pay the mortgage. Within a year, it expanded into an adjoining building. Within ten years, Alford's twenty percent had made him a wealthy man. Today, there's a Corey's department store in half the malls in the state.

But if Corey's was how Tolliver's father made his fortune, it was the fight against the electric utility that made his legend.

In the first third of this century, electrical utilities were cash machines. The industry operated virtually without government oversight: it generated the power, erected the lines, provided electricity only in areas it wanted (meaning where there was a big industrial customer or lots of homes clumped together), and charged what it wanted. When farmers asked that power lines be strung to their areas, they were either charged an absurdly high fee or refused outright. It's little wonder, then, that as late as 1935, only one in ten of the nation's farms had electricity.

Like all good robber barons, though, the utility tycoons weren't happy with merely getting rich. They wanted to control the whole industry. So in the 1920s, they set out to corner the market by buying up electrical companies.

They might have succeeded, too, but for two things. One was that they overplayed their hand, making such a naked grab for riches that they annoyed the holy hell out of everyone including Franklin Roosevelt, who made it his personal mission to break the utilities. The other thing was something called the Wilson Dam at Muscle Shoals, Alabama.

The dam had been built by the federal government during World War I to provide power to a nitrate plant proposed for the spot. Nitrate is used to make explosives, and the government needed some big boomers to lob at the filthy Huns. But the war ended before the project was finished, so the power plant was mothballed and sat idle for fifteen years or so while everyone argued about what to do with it.

Some politicians thought the facility should be operated by the government to provide inexpensive power to the Tennessee River valley. Utility company executives thought it should be sold or, preferably, given to private industry because the government had no right to tinker with the free market. When the market decides it's time for farmers to have power, they'll have it, the executives declared, and not a moment sooner.

Even Henry Ford got into the fray, briefly. Ford offered to buy the facility and make it the cornerstone of an ambitious plan to develop the whole valley. That plan, and Ford's presidential hopes, both enjoyed a heyday in the early 1920s, until Congress took a close look at the deal he was proposing: that he pay a paltry $5 million for the Muscle Shoals facility, and then only if the government sank another $68 million into the project. Ford's offer was refused and he slunk back to Michigan, where he cemented his reputation as a half-crazy old coot by spending the rest of his life raving about the Jews.

Roosevelt ended the debate by creating the Tennessee Valley Authority in 1933. Muscle Shoals' generators were dusted off and cranked up, and cheap power began flowing. But that solved only one problem. It broke the electric industry's monopoly on power, but it still didn't get electricity to farmers.

So a couple of years later, Roosevelt created the Rural Electrification Administration, which loaned money to rural cooperatives to help farmers pay for stringing power lines. One of the first co-ops was formed in Soque County, in which Barrington is located. This is where Alford Tynan enters the tale.

The Soque Electric Co-op was one of the REA's early success stories. The financing came through quickly, poles went up, substations were built, and the TVA routed power over the north Georgia hills with a minimum of fuss. By 1937, the farms closest to Barrington had power in place and the grid was expanding by the day. Only one thing marred this happy scene: when the city mice found out how little the country mice were paying for power, their whiskers trembled in outrage.

So the city mice went to North Georgia Electric, the Barrington power company, and asked that prices be reduced. The company's answer was couched in long explanations about capital investment and amortization of debt, but when boiled down, it was this: Bugger off.

Thus began a grueling eighteen-month legal battle between the company and a citizens' group led by Alford. The group first asked North Georgia Electric to sell its system—poles, wires, substations, everything—to the city, which could then buy cheap TVA power itself. The company, naturally enough, didn't wish to sell and claimed its investment to date was so high that the city couldn't afford to buy the system. Al-

139

ford did his own calculations and determined that most of North Georgia Electric's investment had already been recovered through its monopolistic rate setting, and that much of the value the company placed on the system couldn't really be measured: stuff like projections of future use. The company said it didn't care for either Mr. Tynan or his silly calculations, it wasn't selling and that was that.

Except that wasn't that. Alford the lawyer did some research and determined that the city could use its power of eminent domain to condemn and seize the system. Alford the businessman determined that the city could sell bonds to compensate the company for the seized system, and pay off those bonds through a levy on every consumer. Alford the salesman convinced voters that even with that levy, the low cost of TVA power meant the money they spent on electricity would be reduced. And Alford the private citizen was first in line at the polling place on election day, when Barrington's voters overwhelmingly approved a referendum on the whole matter.

So the city seized the system. North Georgia Electric was left with only one weapon, and it used it immediately. The day after condemnation was completed, it sued the city over the appraised price of the system, hoping to drive it so high that the city would have second thoughts. The city council—figuring you stick with the guy who brought you to the dance—hired Alford to face the company in court.

But North Georgia Electric made two serious mistakes. It got a change of venue in the trial, on the theory that no impartial jury could be found among the citizens of Soque County. The trial was moved down the road forty miles or so—to Athens, Alford's hometown. Also, the company made the classic corporate misstep of hiring a handful of hotshot Atlanta lawyers to rub Alford's nose in the ground in front of his friends and former neighbors.

It could not have been worse for the company. When it sought to use the original per-mile cost of building the system to establish its value, Alford convinced the judge to use instead the TVA's average per-mile cost, on the theory that the city was required to pay only a fair market value, not past costs—and unfortunately for the company, the cost of building a system had dropped dramatically in recent years. When the company introduced appraisals for the real estate it owned, Alford showed that the appraisals were conducted by a subsidiary of North Georgia Electric, and that the subsidiary's previous estimates of the value of the land had been much lower when the utility was a buyer, not a seller. And when the company tried to set a value on its administrative functions—billing, record keeping, and so forth—Alford showed that all those tasks actually had been performed by yet another subsidiary at an astonishingly high price, which had then been merely passed along to Barrington's consumers.

As the news reports in the *Barrington Chronicle* made clear, the case was lost early. While the jurors may not have been customers of North Georgia Electric—and therefore presumably not biased against it—they also had no reason to kowtow to the company. And in the eyes of the jury, Alford's triumphs were magnified by the difference between the aw-shucks local boy fighting for the average joe and the formal Atlanta lawyers who were, in essence, demanding that the utility be granted one last rape of the consumer. When the jury finally got the case, it deliberated a long time; as it turned out, some jurors wanted to give the company even less than Alford estimated the system was worth. But the judge reminded them that they were arbiters, not appraisers, and when the verdict came in, the city of Barrington was awarded the system for exactly the price Alford had set.

For three days, Alford was a hero. People stopped him on

the street to shake his hand and the *Chronicle* lionized him in an editorial. He'd not only put money in people's pockets, he'd engineered a popular uprising against a hated corporation. There was talk of sending him to the state legislature.

On the fourth day, Alford passed into sainthood. On his way back from Athens—where he had picked up a signed copy of the judge's order setting the system's price—Alford swerved his car to avoid hitting some livestock on the road and collided with a tree. It's said that when his body was found, he was holding the order in his hand.

Here's what Alford left behind:

Maddie, his wife, was pregnant with their daughter, who was born days after his death. Tallasee Tynan grew up to be a remarkable young woman with all the compassion Tolliver lacked.

Corey's Clothes had already made Alford a millionaire, and its continued growth swelled his estate over the years. At the time of her death, Maddie was worth over $20 million; her heirs still own twenty percent of the company, which has branched into shopping center development and real estate investment trusts.

Tolliver Tynan, ten years old when Alford died, grew to be a handsome young man, often hearing himself compared favorably to his father. But when I first met him, I was unencumbered by history; I didn't know who his daddy was, so it didn't figure into my judgment of him. Where others saw in Tolliver a youthful, if occasionally wayward, high-spiritedness, I saw a strange glitter in his eyes as he tormented me. He's been rotten all his life, and it's just his bad luck I finally got a chance to say so.

◆ ◆ ◆

You should by now have the sense that Tolliver had a certain roguish charm. This was not an acquired trait; even in his earliest days, he cut a wide path through hearts, beginning with his mother's. By the time he hit eighteen, he'd ridden that charm through school, past a couple of minor encounters with police officers, and into the warm, slick embrace of several girls. He'd gotten his father's easy smile and grace, but none of his baggage of ambition or responsibility. There's a point in life, however, when charm doesn't stand on its own any longer, when it fails to mask shortcomings. Tolliver had reached that point when he began dating Lucinda Haysfield.

Lucinda was everything that Tolliver wasn't. Where he was unemployed and without apparent plans to ever work, she had a job as a saleswoman at Corey's department store and had been accepted to the teachers college in Statesboro. Where he rarely went to church, she led a youth group and sang in the choir. Where he had only one parent, and treated that one badly, she came from a loving family and obeyed her parents. Where he was brash, careless, and promiscuous, she was bashful, careful, and virginal. She was the girl you hoped your son would bring home; he was the boy you feared your daughter would fall for. Lucinda and Tolliver seemed to be the classic romantic formula: The good girl falls for the bad boy, finds his inner goodness, and turns him away from his life of trouble and degradation.

But the formula doesn't account for the effect of alcohol, the freedom of a car, and the betrayal of the body as it feels a bold hand on its secret spots. Tolliver found that small seed of corruption that lives in even the most virtuous, and made it grow.

So for a time, the two of them were often seen together at the roadhouses, dance halls, and cafes that could only nestle against the Soque County line in those days before people realized it was better to tax sin than to deny its existence. Those who knew Tolliver figured the relationship wouldn't last; those who knew Lucinda hoped it wouldn't. Both groups got their wish.

One cloudy night, when the mist had gathered in the low spots on the roads and a film of moisture covered everything, a man driving on U.S. 441 north of Barrington came upon a car accident. The car was overturned in the ditch beside the road, with its headlights still shining spookily into the trees. The man later told police that he found the driver sitting on the edge of the highway with his head in his hands, blood running down his arms from several bad cuts. It was Tolliver. He responded to a shake on the shoulder, confirmed that he could walk, and let himself be led to the good Samaritan's truck and driven to the hospital. The sheriff's report noted that the truck driver said Tolliver reeked of liquor and that a hospital nurse had described him as "a drunken mess" when she tried to get him to tell her about possible internal injuries. Later that evening, a sheriff's deputy drove to the scene of the accident to meet a tow truck, and only after the car was righted and winched out of the ditch was Lucinda's body found. Tolliver was charged with vehicular homicide that night and jailed.

Sometime before dawn, Jesus signed on as Tolliver's defense attorney.

At his preliminary hearing the next day, the judge asked: "Do you wish to enter a plea at this time?"

"The Lord has told me not to sit in judgment," Tolliver replied.

"The court will enter a plea of not guilty on the defendant's behalf," the judge said. "Have you consulted a lawyer, Mr. Tynan?"

"I don't need help to answer man's law. The Lord has told

me to accept judgment gladly and concentrate on doing his good work. Whatever you decide in your wisdom is fine with me, sir."

The judge sighed. "Mr. Tynan, this is not a trial. We are here only to see if the evidence warrants the charge against you and to hear your plea. This is a serious charge, and I suggest you take it seriously."

"My work for the Lord is also serious, sir," Tolliver said, speaking loudly. By now, all the whispered conversations between court officials that go on during routine proceedings had stopped. Everyone was listening.

"I know a little about you, Mr. Tynan, and I have to say that you've kept your interest in doing the Lord's work well hidden," the judge said. "I would hate to think that your possible role in the death of a young lady has anything to do with this interest."

"It's not an interest, sir. It's a life's commitment."

"Very well, Mr. Tynan. I'm going to schedule you for trial and release you into the custody of your mother. My advice is that you seek the help of an attorney as soon as possible. The Lord may be a comfort to you at this moment, but he's not a member of the bar, as far as I know."

"May He forgive you for your blasphemy, sir," Tolliver said.

The funny thing is, it worked. By the time Tolliver came to trial six weeks later, almost everyone was convinced that a genuine conversion had occurred. He never deviated and never passed up an opportunity to proclaim his faith. He took to carrying a Bible with him everywhere and began innumerable sentences with the phrase "As Jesus taught us . . ." The earnest look never left his face.

But there was an important element missing from this

pose. Never once did Tolliver admit responsibility or express regret for the accident. Most people were too captivated by what was unfolding before them to notice. Everyone agreed that Tolliver had killed Lucinda; the only debate was how much his new faith should factor into the punishment. Consequently, when the trial began, no one was prepared for Tolliver's defense.

First, his attorney established that it was unproven that Tolliver was drunk the night of the accident. No one, it turned out, had given Tolliver what's called a field sobriety test—walking in a straight line, touching his nose with his finger, and so on. The defense attorney didn't dispute that Tolliver smelled of alcohol, but noted that it could have been spilled on his clothes at some point during the evening. And the emergency room nurse conceded on the stand that what she had called a drunken stupor could have been the result of having his brains rattled in the accident.

Then Tolliver took the stand and offered up the real shocker: Lucinda had killed herself. He hadn't been driving at all, he claimed.

It was a masterful performance. He mixed the candor of a reformed sinner with the regret of a lover forced to spill secrets. Indeed, he had introduced Lucinda to a life of vice and sin, he admitted. But under questioning—and not without some well-timed squirms and evasions that made his own attorney sound like a prosecutor as he bored in on the "truth"— he said Lucinda had taken to that life a little too enthusiastically; she had decided she liked dancing and drinking and the feel of a fast car. He'd grown alarmed at this change, Tolliver said, because he'd already heard the Lord's call and was having trouble breaking from his life of sin. But instead of helping him out, she was pulling him back in.

Tolliver testified that on the night of the accident, he'd

told Lucinda that the two of them had no future, and she had become distraught at the news and demanded that they leave the roadhouse they were visiting. As they left, she asked if she could drive his car, as one last memory of the time they'd spent together (which included his teaching her how to drive). She'd driven too fast and carelessly, even crazily, Tolliver testified, and ignored his pleas to slow down; finally, she steered off the road in an apparently deliberate effort to kill them both that only half succeeded.

The prosecutor, caught unawares by Tolliver's tale, fumbled his cross-examination. He asked a few feeble questions that Tolliver easily answered, then recalled some witnesses to the stand only to find that no one had actually asked Tolliver if he was driving that night. In the end, he was reduced to excoriating Tolliver in his closing argument, damning him for "this unconscionable soiling of a dead girl's reputation, this repugnant slander of someone who isn't here to defend herself against the vile charges we've heard." But the cascade of adjectives didn't register with the jury, which took only thirty-five minutes to return a not-guilty verdict. Clutching his Bible and smiling broadly, Tolliver stepped outside the courtroom and declared that God's imprimatur surely now had been placed on his life.

It didn't have to end like that. Had the prosecutor interviewed the truck driver who first came upon the accident—who happened to be Archibald Thacker—he'd have had the testimony he needed.

"That boy told me he just lost control on the curve," I heard Arch say years later. "I kept him talking on the ride to the hospital, 'cause I was afraid he'd die on me if he went quiet. He told me exactly what happened, and he was driving. No question.

"I called the police station later and asked if I was supposed to talk to somebody about all this. Some dumb-ass cop told me that if they needed anything else, they'd find me. It was clear they didn't need some old nigger's help.

"And I'll tell you something else. He never said a word about that girl being in the car with him. He just kept talking about how much he'd messed up his car. He left her to die."

Is it any wonder I hate him? I never got another valentine from Lucinda. My one love, distant as she was, died at Tolliver's hands in a water-filled ditch on a lonely country road.

Tolliver's got good follow-through. I have to give him that.

I won't pretend that I know exactly why he continued this charade of blessedness, but either of two possibilities is likely: He figured it was necessary to keep public opinion on his side, or he discovered that the ministry was a wonderful job—no heavy lifting, minimal scholarship requirements, automatic influence over local events, and great benefits like a house, a car, and providing special comfort to young widows. Knowing Tolliver, I suspect it began as the first and evolved into the second.

He enrolled at Barrington Baptist College, where his intelligence and his touched-by-tragedy history—not just Lucinda, remember, but his father as well—moved him to the front of the class, both academically and emotionally. His touch remained flawless. He played the role of convert perfectly, never referring to the accident directly but also making sure everyone remembered that his conversion wasn't the garden-variety come-to-Jesus burst of enlightenment. His was born of pain and sacrifice, and by the time he graduated, everyone had forgotten that the pain and sacrifice had all been borne by someone else.

In the summer of 1953, he was picked to preach the summer revival at Barrington Baptist. At the end of that revival week, he was asked to stay on as an associate minister. In 1958, upon the retirement of the church's resident shepherd, Tolliver was named minister, giving him the house, the car, and the status, influence, and popularity. The only thing he didn't have was money; thanks to the terms of Alford's estate, his mother still controlled the family fortune, and in her addle-brained, prattle-tongued way, old Maddie was too smart to entrust it to Tolliver. So he eventually began looking for investment opportunities, which led him first to Percy Queen, then to Ike Enheer & Associates, and finally to ruin.

From the distance of the years, it's clear that Tolliver's career in the ministry ended much the same way as it began: one death marked its start, and another marked its finish.

After several attempts, Perry Ray Pruitt finally got the torch lit, and Tolliver held it aloft. The crowd had gathered in a half-circle around the truck trailer where the two of them stood behind a makeshift pulpit. They'd already been warmed up by Perry Ray—or, considering his aptitude for it, cooled down by Perry Ray—and now it was Tolliver's turn. The television crews switched on their lights, and the newspaper and magazine photographers closed in. The faithful pressed in as well, with teenagers clutching records to their bosoms and the occasional parent holding a book to be hurled into the fire. Tolliver, standing in his shirtsleeves with tie loosened, sleeves rolled up, and a lock of hair curled over his forehead, cut a telegenic figure; even the torch performed famously, burning strong and bright above Tolliver's head. He stood still as death, waiting for the crowd to fall silent. When the murmuring and shuffling finally settled down, he spoke.

"It is indeed tragic that the person who needs to be here the most isn't," Tolliver declared. "But it is indeed joyful to see you all here tonight, to help me make this declaration of faith before the eyes of the world.

"We are here to reclaim our kingdom for our God. We are here to beat back the forces that would take our children from us, and lead them into a life of sin and debasement. We are here to tell the purveyors of filth that the line has been drawn in the sand, and that they cross it at their own risk. We are here to deliver a clear message: No mortal man is more popular than our Lord Jesus Christ.

"We are here to light up the night with our righteousness."

Tolliver paused. His arm held the torch steady as a light breeze snapped off the ends of the flame.

"I'm not here tonight to deliver a sermon. This is a time for action, not talk. Help me now spread the light of Christianity around the globe."

Sometimes I think I was present for the birth of the sound bite. Tolliver had spoken for less than a minute, and the television cameras had recorded every second of it. He'd figured that this was the moment for a gut punch, not a debate of the issue, and he delivered it adroitly. And cleverest of all, he never once used the word "fire." Despite the fact that a mob of otherwise decent and sober citizens was about to destroy thousands of books and records, this was not destruction. It was illumination.

In fact, were it not for what happened next, I suspect Tolliver's little speech would have been rebroadcast word for word. Instead, it was forgotten when what he said became less interesting than what he did.

Holding the torch carefully above his head, Tolliver stepped down from the truck trailer and walked to the pile of lumber I'd stacked that afternoon. As the crowd edged closer, he jammed the torch into the middle of the stack; the kindling caught fire almost immediately, and within a few moments the flames had fully taken root. One of the television cameramen clambered onto the truck trailer, giving him a high angle on the events that later would be shown so many times.

I must have a knack for pyrotechnics. I'd used every scrap of lumber that had been dumped in the church parking lot, and I'd apparently hit the precise air-to-combustible-material formula in the stacking. The fire blazed up so hot that the crowd was forced to fall back. Only Tolliver stood his ground, throwing his right hand in the air and shouting: "Who will be the first to deliver the message?"

A great cry went up, and hundreds of records and books sailed through the air into the fire. It continued steadily for the next few minutes as the people from the back of the crowd worked their way to the front to offer up their vinyl sacrifice. I even saw Tallasee edging toward the flames, two records in her hand. When she got close, I could see both were albums by Frank Sinatra.

She caught my eye and shrugged sheepishly. "They're my mother's," she said, and tossed them in. "I always hated him."

Somewhere, a voice began singing "Onward, Christian Soldiers." Others joined in, and soon everyone was braying as best their lungs would allow. In the middle of the chorus, the huge log I'd stood on end in the middle of the stack burned through near the bottom. It fell on its side, sending a tall chimney of sparks and blazing chips into the air, carried aloft by the intense heat.

The devil was about to work his mischief.

13

It doesn't make sense, in a way. You spend years hating a woman who abandoned you on a bus, leaving you behind on the seat like an empty soft-drink bottle, yet twenty-five years later you end up riding those very same buses—or at least their younger cousins—across two states trying to find her.

I began looking in 1965. I'd given up my membership in the Athens chapter of the Wick Dippers Club after Jenkins died, and had fallen into the habit of spending one day a week in the Barrington Public Library. I would arrive early, stake out a chair near the window that overlooked the lawn, gather an armload of books and magazines chosen with a deliberate randomness, and settle in for the day. As a result, I'll be able to chatter on with the best of them if I'm ever invited to a cocktail party: the French New Wave cinema, this fresh young author Updike, the Negro civil rights movement, the domino theory of foreign policy, DDT, Cheever versus O'Hara, and the wisdom of adding a few more military advisers in Vietnam. Of course, all this presupposes that social issues have remained unchanged since the early 1960s, and that cocktail party chatter doesn't actually require me to talk.

The self-help industry was already afoot by then, so I also dipped into the psychology texts. The messages were pretty clear: Be good to yourself. Don't internalize your anger. Share your feelings. Get in touch with your true self. Embrace honesty and self-awareness. The more I read, the more I realized that what I really wanted in life was to get in touch with my feelings by finding my mother and slapping the hell out of her. So I began searching.

In the beginning, it was all research. I knew a few simple facts. We had boarded a bus in Birmingham one afternoon in 1940 and I had stepped off that same bus about thirteen hours later in Barrington. I was sure it was spring, because I remembered the early-morning chill before the heat of the sun settled in on me as I sat on that bus station bench the first day; probably just after Easter, because I had a faint memory of being given a basket with colored eggs shortly before we left Alabama. I remembered a number of stops in small towns before I went to sleep, and I could presume there were others throughout the night. And I remembered that the driver who nudged me awake in Barrington was different from the one who'd begun the trip, meaning there'd been a change sometime during the night.

A few minutes with a road atlas gave me a reasonable stab at the route: U.S. Highway 78 from Birmingham to Atlanta, then U.S. 23 north from Atlanta to Barrington. It was 350 miles, as best I could determine, and the path was dotted with dozens of small towns—many of which would have been stops on a bus route in 1940. My first task, then, was to find a bus schedule from that era listing the towns where we would have stopped.

For lack of a better idea, I planned to simply travel to

those towns and scan back issues of the local newspaper from that fateful month. What else could I do? A couple of decades later, television's *Unsolved Mysteries* or one of its kin could have done the job for me: "Tonight we have the story of a boy who became tragically separated from his mother . . ." Then, presumably, one of the sharp-eyed snoops whose nosiness has been made legitimate by these shows would identify my mother, and a later show would air some heartwarming film footage of me confronting her and breaking a lifelong silence to tell her what a selfish slut she was, hopefully accompanied by a gut punch or two. But at the time, I was left to my own devices, and newspapers seemed like a logical place to begin. I didn't know exactly what I was looking for; it's not as if wayward mothers are in the habit of dropping by the local newspaper office and announcing that they've just abandoned their sons at the bus station, and are now available for a quick feature story. I was hoping for a clue of some kind. I had no sense that her leaving me on the bus was part of a deliberate effort. My gut told me it was done on impulse, that one night she just liberated herself. But I remembered that she was almost penniless—she couldn't even afford two bus tickets—and a single, destitute woman in a strange town could well find herself sitting on her groceries. So, I reasoned, she could have turned up in a newspaper roundup of arrest reports.

Getting a bus schedule from 1940 proved to be a chore. I rifled through McAdoo's desk drawers one night, but found nothing. I located the box that held Jenkins's files; again, nothing. I tried the library, but the old bat in charge of research just shrugged helplessly when I handed her my written request. I even invented a vice president of Ike Enheer & Associates and had him write the bus company, but when the answer came, it said that only current routes are discussed and that past or future routes are considered proprietary information. So in the end, I guessed that she'd disappeared somewhere between Atlanta and Birmingham, and made a list of the twenty-five towns my map showed as dots along that route—international ports of call like Villa Rica, Georgia, and Estaboga, Alabama. I set out to visit them.

I was able to arrange, and afford, about one trip every other month. I would typically catch the last bus out of Barrington for Atlanta, then cool my heels in the Atlanta depot until the Birmingham-bound bus left early the next morning. The first four trips were uniformly useless. On the initial trip, I rode only as far as the first stop, spent the day in the local library thumbing fruitlessly through a couple of months' worth of the local paper, caught the last bus to Atlanta, and spent a second evening catnapping on a bench before returning to Barrington the next morning. On the second trip, I got off at the second stop and repeated the whole exercise. Third and fourth trips, ditto. While I was learning an enormous amount about local sports heroes and the meeting habits of small-town garden clubs, the newspapers hadn't served up a single useful clue.

But at the start of my fifth trip, I got some unexpected help from the ticket agent in Atlanta who had sold me my previous fares.

"You're getting to be a regular customer," she said. I nodded.

"How come you make all those short trips?" she asked. I shrugged.

"Don't talk much, do you?" she said. The depot was nearly empty and, with no one behind me in line, she had time to kill. I tapped my ear and shook my head.

"You can't hear?" she said. She was middle-aged and goggle-eyed, with lots of poofed-out hair piled on top of her head. "You sure seem to understand everything I say."

I shrugged again.

"I'll bet you'll be back here tomorrow, huh? I've seen you sitting overnight, trying to pretend you're not sleeping. We're not supposed to let people sleep overnight, but if they sit up and don't cause trouble, we let 'em snooze. So what's the story? You got a girlfriend somewhere?"

I shook my head. Suddenly, it occurred to me that she might be able to help. Fishing a pencil out of my pocket, I wrote a question on the small pad I always carry: "How long have you worked here?"

"I've been here thirty years, on and off," she said. "Are you deaf? I've never talked to a dummy before."

I nodded as I wrote again: "Do you have bus schedules from 1940 here?"

Her lips moved slightly as she read. "Nah, we wouldn't have anything that old. What do you want it for?"

I wrote: "Where did drivers change then between Birmingham and Atlanta?"

"Well, even back then, they usually drove straight through. But we used to have a big depot in Anniston, and sometimes they switched there. The company didn't like it, though. There was a honky-tonk across the street, even though it's a dry county, and when drivers got off shift, they'd go over. So they stopped changing drivers there." Her mouth became prim. "It won't do to have drivers drinking in public, you know."

I felt a tickle at the edge of my brain.

I found the old bus station on a decaying edge of Anniston's small downtown. I'd spotted it on the way into the city, a few blocks from the new depot, as the bus wound its way through the streets, and walked directly there. It was the twin of Barrington's station: the same cinder block construction, the same transom windows, the same parking layout, and—I was willing to bet—the same interior storeroom. The door was boarded up and weeds had grown through cracks in the asphalt. On the wall facing the street someone had written "MOVED WEST THREE BLOCKS" in lopsided spray-painted letters, with an off-kilter arrow pointing the way.

Across the street, the old cafe was a matched piece, also boarded and deserted. But I could see how it would have been a magnet years before, as country boys, soldiers from nearby Fort McClellan, and thirsty drivers got off their buses, heard the music and saw the neon glow from just across the street. It had the look, even in its decayed state, of a place that police officers both loathe and appreciate for its ability to simultaneously breed and contain trouble. It's little wonder that the bus line made sure that few of its drivers ended their shifts there; like the ticket agent said, the sight of a uniformed driver stumbling out of a honky-tonk or standing in a police lineup after a brawl tends to register firmly in the bus-riding public's consciousness.

I sat on the curb in front of the deserted cafe, facing the bus station, and dredged my memory. We'd boarded the bus in Birmingham late in the afternoon, perhaps a half hour before dusk. I remembered night falling as we rolled through the countryside. Anniston was perhaps seventy miles from Birmingham, which meant that once stops were figured in, we'd been on the bus at least two hours before it had stopped here to collect other riders and change drivers. So if I had no memory of this place, it wasn't unexpected; the droning of the bus and the quickening darkness had put me to sleep long before the bus arrived here. But if none of it looked familiar, it felt right. I would learn something here.

After about thirty minutes, I stood, brushed off the seat of my pants, and trudged downtown. It was time to start slogging through newspapers.

The woman behind the desk at the library looked at me

over the top of her glasses when I slid my request toward her. She frowned while she read, then said: "I'll point them out to you, but you'll have to get them off the shelf yourself. They're too big for me to lift."

We walked to the rear of the library where, against the back wall, there were giant newspaper-sized volumes stacked upright, with their months and years stamped in gold on the spines. "Take any of them down, but just leave them on the table when you're done," the woman said. "And don't cut anything out. These aren't scrapbooks."

I nodded, and she left. I found the volume labeled "Jan–June 1940" and pulled it from the shelf, laying it flat on the large table. The cover crackled when I opened it. By the time I'd thumbed through the January newspapers, I knew where the local news articles were grouped. By the time I got through February and March, I was fairly flying through the classified ads, sports scores, and wedding announcements. By the time I got into April, I'd found her.

*Truth be told, I almost missed it altogether. I was looking for an ar*rest report or some other item carrying the name Lilly Ayers, and had already turned several pages past the article before something registered and I thumbed back.

There, under a headline that said: "Woman Found Dead," was the announcement of my birth as a parentless, speechless, small-town oddity:

> *The body of a young woman was found Thursday morning in an empty lot on Anniston's south side.*
> *Police officials said it appeared the woman had been strangled. No other details were available. The body was found by a Negro trash-picker in the lot adjoining*

Aubrey's Cafe, across the street from the Anniston bus depot, police said.

The unidentified woman was wearing a red silk blouse and appeared to be in her mid- to late twenties, police said. Patrons of Aubrey's told investigators that an attractive woman fitting that description had been seen leaving the cafe with a soldier Wednesday evening.

Detectives said they have asked base officials at Fort McClellan to supply a list of all personnel who have been granted leave during the week.

Anyone with information about the identity of the victim is asked to contact the Anniston police department.

The rest of the story was laid out as I scanned the next several weeks' worth of papers. Every enlisted man stationed at Fort McClellan who had leave that day was questioned—it wasn't clear why officers were exempted from the interrogations; presumably because they order the murder of civilians, not commit it—and a suspect was identified. In the course of a session with detectives, the soldier gave a detailed confession and subsequently pleaded guilty to murder. His story was ordinary and casually violent: She was a real looker, he was a little drunk, he bought her a drink and they talked, she said she had to catch a bus and made ready to leave, he got angry when he realized his investment of a drink wasn't going to see any return and she was something of a tease besides, he went out with her, yanked her around the corner of the cafe, hit her in the face when she started to scream, hit her again so hard she fell to the ground, then raped and strangled her, all within the shadow of the building not ten paces from the sidewalk. He hadn't meant for any of it to happen and he felt real sorry about it, but what was a good-looking woman doing in a place like that if not to keep America's fighting men happy?

The newspaper, working hard to keep a good story alive, focused on the victim's identity. Headline writers dubbed her the Woman in the Red Blouse and the Luckless Lass. For a couple of weeks, there was a spirited effort to find her family. Sheriff's deputies visited the tenant farms that dotted the countryside to ask if a young woman had set out from any of them to seek her way in the world. Other police agencies were notified and bulletins were mailed out. A sketch was made and published in the newspaper under a headline that asked: "Do You Know This Woman?"

No one did. After a while, other events overtook the story, pushing it to the inside pages and eventually out of the paper altogether. I found the last article buried deep in the paper, a three-paragraph notice published five weeks after her murder:

MYSTERY VICTIM LAID TO REST

The unidentified woman whose body was found in a trash-strewn south side lot was buried in a pauper's grave Monday, after a long effort to find her family proved unsuccessful.

The woman was strangled after she left Aubrey's Cafe on the evening of April 4. A soldier from Fort McClellan has been charged with her murder. He has already given investigators a detailed account of the killing, police said.

A marker for the grave was donated by the Anniston Police Auxiliary.

Everything fit—the blouse, the age, the sketch, the location and the time. I could even see how it happened: When the bus pulled in to pick up passengers and swap drivers, there probably was a half hour or so of idle time. From the bus window, she could see the honky-tonk's lights, perhaps even hear the music; I could imagine her shifting restlessly in her seat, fidgeting with the jacket that had been thrown over me as a blanket, then finally deciding to just go over for a few minutes. She probably convinced herself that she needed to stretch her legs a bit, was just going across the street, for gosh sakes, to sit by the cafe's window and not even be out of eyeshot of the bus. She was a social creature, I knew. My existence testified to that. She was also probably lonely and bored and panicky in the way that having a child too young and feeling the juice seep out of you year by year can make you. And something had worried her enough to put us in full flight on a bus, headed for God knows where, at a time when she couldn't even afford two tickets. Walking thirty yards across the street and letting a man buy her a drink while she waited for her bus to leave may have been a lapse in judgment, but she didn't deserve the death penalty for it.

Damn those psychology texts. How was I supposed to maintain any rage in my life if I began to see her as a victim? I wanted an old woman whose life I could make miserable with guilt in her last years.

I've always liked a good cemetery. Where else would I be considered the loud, fun-loving one?

I spend a fair bit of time in the Barrington Municipal Waste Yard and Landfill, tending to Jenkins's grave. Its official name is Memorial Cemetery, but that's too somber a name for my taste; if you can't make fun of death, what's the point of living? Most folks have a misguided attitude about death, as if treating it respectfully will somehow ward it off. It won't, as several billion people have learned the hard way. As often as not, it's the happy end to a wretched life. When I sat on the whorehouse floor and blubbered after finding Jenkins's body, I was crying for myself, not him. He didn't have anything to be upset about—he was rejoining his family, and he'd died with his spoon in hand. The only thing sad about it was that his last mortal emotion likely was shame, knowing he was being stricken in midsnack, with half his oysters left in the jar at bedside for someone to find.

The world is a rotten, treacherous, and evil place. It finds countless ways to humiliate you while you're alive, then finishes you off in a hurry if you're doing something fun, like Jenkins was, or stretches out your demise if you're in terrible pain. I don't understand this reverence for life. I've had perhaps ten minutes of unadulterated happiness in my life, total. And probably half of that came from watching Tolliver's face on the two occasions when he realized what I'd done to him. If anyone tells you they've had more than a day's worth of happiness in their life—that the moments of calm and unconcern added up to more than twenty-four hours—then they're liars. It can't happen. The world parcels out happiness in seconds-long increments. Why do you think Christianity has such currency? It holds out heaven as the place where you can finally relax and stop worrying about the rent payment, that lump in your breast, the 105-degree fever in the middle of a child's night, the mysterious clunk in the transmission, the new boss, the old recurring arguments with your spouse, the phone that rings at three A.M. when Junior's still out with the car, that misshapen mole on your back, Muslim terrorists, the high-voltage power lines behind the house, tooth decay, drugs, guns, disease, and a Republican majority in Congress.

Anniston's boneyard reminded me of Barrington's. It had the same wrought-iron picket fence along its border facing the road, an asphalt path that meandered about, great oaks whose roots had tilted some of the older gravestones, and a weedy look born of municipal budget cuts that makes a park seem unkempt but a cemetery somehow friendly. I knew it would be segregated just like Barrington's—black folks buried in a far corner, a cluster of expensive monuments front and center, and the poor whites assigned to something in between—so it didn't take me long to find her.

The gravestone was small, no bigger than the ones put at the foot of a rich man's grave, and rounded off at the top. It said simply: "Unknown woman. Died April 4, 1940."

I squatted down beside the grave and picked at the stray twigs and leaves that littered it. The settling of the earth above the coffin had caused the gravestone to lean forward a few degrees, pulling it inexorably into the ground. Around it were a few other paupers' graves, marked only with large rocks. The branches of a nearby tree had grown over the years to keep the spot shaded most of the day, meaning what grass there was had an anemic look. It was the cemetery's forgotten edge; I was likely the first person in years to visit the place who wasn't there by accident or to dig.

I sat for most of the afternoon thinking about her, shifting occasionally to warm myself in the patches of sunlight that filtered through the trees. I know what I'm supposed to do at this point: I'm supposed to tell you how my heart filled with forgiveness, how I found peace with myself once I knew she didn't deliberately leave me on the bus. I'm supposed to tell you that I purged from my soul all the bile that had caused me to make my life an exercise in punishment—the retribution I'd taken on myself by living in silent exile in a bus depot storeroom, and on others through my deceit and manipulation. Yeah, I could tell you all that. I could wallow in it and have you sobbing quietly to yourself, marveling at how human decency and nobility always prevail. That sort of fraud has a long history in literature. It started early; even Homer couldn't help himself. He had Odysseus' wife Penelope stay chaste for twenty years while the old boy was slaying Trojans and wandering lost around the Aegean. And when he finally finds his way home, he disguises himself as a beggar, confirms that his wife and son have remained pure and purposeful, then kills the swarm of rude layabouts who've been guzzling his booze and pestering his wife to marry one of them.

But this ain't literature; it's truthful life. Homer didn't feel the need to tell the truth, which probably was that Penelope didn't wait more than a few years before shacking up with Zorba from the next village, and that Odysseus junior kept the sheep in a state of terror. But I'm telling you what really happened, and in truthful life, forgiveness doesn't come easily. I didn't want to stop hating her. My desire for her return that first summer had been an open wound, exposed and raw, and when it finally healed it had closed over something hard. I had come to think of that hard thing as my strength: it was a fist-sized rock in my belly that set me apart from weaker, louder beings. Going all soft and gooey while squatting next to my mother's grave would be contrary to that strength. It wasn't the end I wanted. She didn't abandon me after all, but so what? The result was the same.

But even my strength couldn't stand up to a memory. She had closed the window to shield me from the night's chill. She had kissed me gently. She had whispered comfort in my ear as sleep claimed me. Her memory lived in only one person, and I realized that even I wasn't strong enough to keep hating her. It's hard to hate a weak, pitiful creature who thought her enervating loneliness could be cured by the light and noise of a honky-tonk. She was proof that weakness, disguised in its many forms, is lethal. Talking is weakness. Possessions are weakness. Sex is weakness. Jenkins's guilt was weakness. Perry Ray Pruitt's desire to baptize somebody was weakness. Even Tolliver's need to put a decent face on his corruption was weakness.

Sentiment is weakness too, and I fell prey to it that afternoon. I wanted to mark the end of the search somehow. I already was custodian of one grave, and wasn't in the market to adopt another; besides, it was too far to travel. Also, I wasn't inclined to mark the end of the search by announcing to the newspaper that its long-standing mystery of the Luckless Lass had been solved. Only a fool seeks out the chance to have his life reduced to cheap ironies and a play on words.

It wasn't until I trudged back to the station and boarded the bus for home that I realized what I wanted to do: name her. I would have a proper headstone carved, with her name and birth date, and have it placed on the grave. It was a gesture both simple and permanent. And although I couldn't remember her full name and birth date, I knew how I could find out.

The suitcase was right where I'd put it years before, after retrieving it from locker 9 in the weeks following Jenkins's death. I'd opened it only that one time before pushing it deep to the back of a high shelf in my storeroom, away from any prying eye that might intrude upon my secret. Over the years, other things had been stacked in front of it, pushing it from sight but never from mind.

Its leather was dry and cracked, and the strap came apart in my hand when I tried to yank it free of the buckle. When I opened it, I could smell her on the clothes, an odor from my childhood that brought an unexpected tightening to my throat. She'd packed for a short trip: a few changes of underwear for the two of us, an extra set of clothes for me, and, for her, a second dress, demure and neutral, the sort of outfit you'd wear to demonstrate a seriousness of purpose. There was also a hairbrush and some toilet items; her purse, with two one-dollar bills and some change inside; a torn piece of paper with a

165

phone number written the old way, with two letters at the beginning; and a large manila envelope holding an official document. The envelope contained my treasure.

I copied the information I needed, then sat awake for the rest of the night. Just before dawn, I realized that I'd always assumed I knew whose phone number it was, but had never made sure. I dialed it.

"Hello?" answered a familiar voice, elderly and tremulous. I hung up the phone. Old ladies shouldn't be bothered that early in the morning.

14

Several dozen necks, mine among them, craned upward to watch as the burning embers, carried aloft by the fire's draft, began parachuting back to earth. But I alone, standing at the edge of the crowd and with an ear honed by a lifetime of listening, heard the noise a moment later.

Record albums were still being thrown into the fire as Tolliver shouted his exhortations. Perry Ray Pruitt, until then just a quiet but dogged presence, finally began to be heard from, crowding next to Tolliver on the truck bed to reach the microphone and echoing his phrases in a singsong sort of way.

"May the light burn bright tonight!" Tolliver shouted.

"Burn bright!" Perry Ray repeated.

"Send the message to the world!" Tolliver continued.

"Send the message!" Perry Ray chimed in.

The crowd started picking up on Perry Ray's echo, themselves repeating the phrases he repeated, and you could see him feed on it. He began swaying, leaning into the microphone at the end of Tolliver's sentences and nodding his head to some internal rhythm. After a week of utter failure to inspire the faithful, he finally had them going, and he gave it his all.

It was between the call and the response when I heard it, a muted *whomp* that was almost more of a feeling than a sound. I looked around, but no one else reacted. They would, soon enough.

Seeing Archibald Thacker with a load of moonshine earlier that day brought me even with him when it came to knowing other people's secrets. Until then, he'd been one up on me.

We were the best kind of partners: distrustful and suspicious of one another, but with a common enemy. We were careful to keep our financial affairs from entangling, using lawyers at every point and leaving a clear paper trail that investigators were later only too happy to follow. Of course, Arch was much better at it than I was; being a successful black businessman in a Southern town meant being good at manipulation and deceit. I was the amateur, albeit a willing student with no small talent for deception myself. What I brought to the partnership was the target, Tolliver, and through him the possibility of a little profit. Arch contributed the legal and financial know-how. I was the reason; he was the means.

But I've got to be honest. We never expected it to develop the way it did. We only hoped to nick Tolliver for some money, to make him pay for the right to buy something that he had no real hope of obtaining. That it succeeded beyond my wildest hope—and I call it a success, even though I'm sorry for the suffering it caused—was directly attributable to Perry Ray Pruitt and John Lennon.

Like most things that end badly, it all began with money.

Despite his daddy's riches, Tolliver's never had much money. Percy Queen, the insurance agent, was exactly right when he told the court that old Maddie Tynan was sitting on the fortune. In addition to the twenty percent control of Corey's department stores, the estate consisted of some impressive real estate and stock holdings (including, ironically, a whole handful of utility stocks; Alford Tynan must have concluded that his own triumph over the power barons was an anomaly). Maddie had turned everything over to the trust department of one of Atlanta's largest banks, which—thanks to its judicious flouting of the traditional separation of its trust and lending functions—roughly doubled the fortune by loaning tons of money to Corey's for expansion at precisely the moment America decided that no citizen shall be more than a fifteen-minute drive from a mall. The bank saddled Corey's with an enormous debt that could have threatened the stability of the very estate it was pledged to protect, violating God only knows how many banking regulations over the years. No one complained, however, as the money poured in.

But Maddie didn't spend any of it, either on herself or her children. Her monthly bills, modest as they were, were sent directly to the trust department for payment, and the little cash she needed came from the check sent to her by the bank every other week. She had only two regular out-of-pocket costs: her weekly contribution to the offering plate at Barrington Baptist Church, and her regular payment for yard and handyman work. God and I both work for cash only, preferably up front.

Her children had precisely opposite reactions to the money.

Tallasee couldn't have cared less about it. She wore money lightly and sardonically, much as she wore life itself. It helped, of course, that she was able to live off her looks; she had the Atlanta newspaper to thank for that. One October afternoon when Tallasee was still in high school, the paper sent a reporter and photographer into the hills of north Georgia for the annual fall-comes-to-the-mountains feature story. On the way back from the deep hollows, they stopped at the apple-packing house just outside Barrington, where Tallasee worked on weekends filling sacks with apples and peddling cider. It was a common job for students during the six-week stretch spanning the shift of seasons when the apples were harvested and visitors flocked to the hills for the foliage tour. The photographer spotted Tallasee and asked if she would like to pose for a photo, no doubt hoping that this would be the day when a beautiful young woman finally responded to his leering request with an offer to pose privately for him in the nude. Instead, Tallasee chewed her lip and put on a troubled look before saying, "Gee, I don't know. I should probably ask my dad, but he's in prison. For murder."

But she let him in on the joke with a merry smile, and clambered up the loading dock and posed with a bushel of apples. That photograph was the one played big on the front page of the Sunday paper, and if you saw it you'll understand why the phone at the Tynan house rang not once but twice that very afternoon as the model-agency talent scouts from Atlanta bored in: Tallasee photographed very, very well.

I suppose I should tell you about her fine smile, the butterscotch hair with the natural highlights, the dusting of freckles across the bridge of the nose and upper chest, and the small hands and feet that didn't suggest delicacy nearly as much as precision and efficiency. And if I were any sort of man, I would describe her body in effusive detail, tell of the fullness and shape that she carried without a shred of self-consciousness. But I won't, because Tallasee herself placed little stock in all that. Besides, I've never even told you what I look like; why should I go on about Tallasee? So you can make her the star of some sick little fantasy?

None of it would convey what the camera was able to capture about her, anyway. That first photograph in the newspaper, like so many of the others that followed in magazines and catalogues, made the eye linger. It made you wonder what she was thinking. That's the real secret, you know; it isn't what the camera is able to show, but what the person being photographed is able to hold back. As she looked out from the front page that Sunday, sitting on an overturned bushel basket, dressed in jeans and an oversized man's white dress shirt rolled up at the sleeves and knotted at the waist, Tallasee made thousands of people wish they'd driven north that weekend and stopped at the apple orchard. Men wanted to talk to her and women wanted to study her. And both groups knew, just from looking at the photograph, that she didn't give a damn what they did—which of course made her even more perversely alluring.

So Tallasee spent the next ten years working as a model. But she's always been an uncommonly intelligent sort, so she didn't bet on it; she worked assignments around her college schedule and graduated with a fine arts degree from the university. She also learned photography in between poses, pestering the shooters about f-stops, shutter settings, and film speed until she understood the nature of light and the equipment that captures it. Then one day, at a point she apparently determined by a formula known to no one else, Tallasee told the modeling agency that she wasn't available any longer, she had quite enough money, thank you, and there's more to life than gazing into a camera and putting on a look that suggests you're dying to give some guy a blow job. With that said, she took her own camera into the remote hills and began collecting photographs and oral histories of the mountain women who'd been born in the years after the Civil War and were coming to the end of lives that hadn't changed much since. You might have seen Tallasee's book. It got rave reviews and sold a

171

whole bunch of copies in cities where career women made sympathetic sounds of solidarity as they thumbed through the pages and convinced themselves that the early skirmishes for survival and equality fought by the wrinkled crones depicted in the book somehow required their latter-day sisters to be childless and predatory.

The book must have made her some money, and the modeling had obviously made her some money, and because she didn't spend much of it on clothes and furniture and the other things that women accumulate, the money made her some money. So, like old Maddie, she had it but didn't much care.

Tolliver, who didn't have any money, cared deeply—which led him first to Percy Queen, then to Archibald Thacker, and finally to Soque circuit court, Judge Bobby Chestnut presiding.

It was Tolliver's bad luck that I got to Archibald first. While he and Percy Queen were engineering their plot to loot the church's insurance fund—and taking their sweet time about it, secure in the belief that with the highway department employee dead and the right-of-way plans safely locked up in Tolliver's desk, they didn't have to hurry—I was writing Eldon Rubicoff with instructions to begin researching the ownership of certain properties. Ike Enheer & Associates, I explained, was considering a move into real estate.

I had some money by then. After twenty years of yardwork, errands, and assorted chores, and by living through barter and charity, I'd accumulated an impressive bit of it. My expenses were few: the broom closet was practically a birthright by then, and McAdoo had given up tormenting me and returned to his first love, which was tormenting Negroes; I still took my meals at Lucille's lunch counter; I still wore Salvation Army haute couture; and if I needed to go anywhere in the county, I usually could hitch a ride on one of Archibald's garbage trucks, squeezing myself in between two of his burly sons or nephews in the cab and pointing out my destination.

I also benefited from the embrace that most Southern towns occasionally offer to their benign eccentrics. For instance, I got my teeth looked after for free, by a dentist who came to the station one morning for a package and asked me to carry it to his car, even though it was light and he was clearly capable of doing it himself. I accepted the fifty-cent tip and was just about to leave when he said, "Hang on there a moment, fella."

I waited. "Do this for me," he said, putting his teeth together and stretching his lips back. I did what he said.

"Now open," he said, yawning his own jaw wide and tilting his head back. Again, I imitated him, letting myself be turned by the shoulders into the sun.

"You're Sammy, right?" he said when he finished looking. I nodded. "I've heard about you. You live here, right? In the bus station? Can you understand me?" I nodded again.

"Well, Sammy, I think we can help each other out. I've got a young hygienist who needs practice and you've got a mouth that hasn't ever seen the sharp end of a dental pick, best as I can tell. You come by my office first thing tomorrow, OK?"

The hygienist was indeed young, but she didn't seem to need practice. And when I left, the woman at the counter gave me a little card with a time written on it for the following week. I got two teeth filled that next visit. Over the next few weeks, I had four more filled. When they were all done, I got a lecture.

"Your teeth are gonna rot, just like anyone else's," the dentist said. "There's a sink somewhere in that bus station, right? You need to get to it, couple of times a day, and brush your teeth. Or next time, we let Jewel"—that was the hygienist—"use sandpaper on those gums."

That was in 1947, and I went back twice a year until the

173

driller retired a few years back. He never asked for payment, so I would sweep up the office parking lot periodically, or trim the shrubs outside the building when they got too ragged. And I had a similar arrangement with the doctor who treated me for walking pneumonia and a couple of nasty cases of the stomach flu. He also tied six stitches in the fleshy part of my palm after I grabbed the jagged edge of a rain gutter when my ladder slipped one day, and set the nose I broke in a Three Stooges–like encounter with a door, putting what looked like a fat knitting needle up each nostril and tugging my head back and forth until he and Lucille agreed my honker was something like its former straight self.

In short, I generally lived for free and traded my labor for anything else I needed. Aside from those years when I traveled to Athens for my monthly dick stretching, I didn't spend money on anything. By the time I recruited Eldon Rubicoff to help me head off McAdoo's campaign to get me out of the station, I'd accumulated $23,133, all in small bills carefully stacked and stored in a pair of shoeboxes on a shelf in my storeroom.

I didn't ease into tycoonhood. Once I decided to spend my money, I did it recklessly, investing on whim and instinct. I'd ridden the bus to Atlanta one morning, shoeboxes tucked under my arm, and opened a checking account at the bank closest to the bus station there, piling the cash up on the teller's counter before a nervous branch manager ushered me into an office to fill out forms. Then, after having consulted the Yellow Pages for an address, I walked over to Peachtree Street and opened an account at a stock brokerage. I gave the broker assigned to me, a bumpkin with cowlicky hair and shrewd eyes, a check for a thousand dollars and a note telling him to park it in his discretionary account until specific investment instructions arrived.

"What exactly do you do, Mr. Ayers?" the broker asked, holding the check in one hand and my instructions in the other.

Rake leaves, I wrote.

He treated it as a joke, laughing heartily as he began the business of filling out new-client forms. When he was done and had pushed them across the desk for me to sign, I noticed that in the square for occupation he'd written: "Professional landscaper."

Thus I became an investor, one of the millions of people with a stake in corporate America. Every few months, I sent the broker a thousand-dollar check and a note telling him to buy a certain stock, picked by any number of methods: I liked the name of the company, I liked its advertising, I liked the way its chief executive officer looked in *Fortune* or *Forbes* magazine, or I liked that he told a labor union or the government or an investment bank to bugger off. Somehow, it worked. I didn't care if I lost money, because I didn't need it to live and it had just been sitting in shoeboxes anyway; so if one of the stocks went into the tank, I didn't feel the need to cut my losses and try to recover them somewhere else. But at the same time, I liked winning, and my quarterly statements from the brokerage were like a scorecard. Each time they arrived, I sat down with a pencil and paper—this was before calculators, mind you, when accounting was so primitive that budgets were actually balanced—and figured the increase of each thousand-dollar investment. Never once did the thousand in the broker's discretionary fund beat my picks.

I got bored with it, though. After picking nineteen stocks, and spending nearly four years doing it, I decided I was tired of reading the financial press. A steady diet of the *Wall Street Journal*, for instance, eventually leaves you with a bizarre filter through which all world events take on a demented cast. Eradication of a disease sparks a sell-off of drug company stocks. Settlement of long-standing hostilities in some remote corner of the world sends arms makers into a blue funk. A famine in the Ukraine pushes wheat futures to record highs. Like the making of sausages, capitalism is one of those things you shouldn't see too closely. It's depressing.

So by the time I overheard the highway department bureaucrat unburden himself to Tolliver, I had a few thousand dollars sitting idle in the bank account. Even though I wasn't interested in real estate speculation, I knew who was; I could practically hear the *cha-ching* of the cash register as Tolliver's conniving mind tallied up the take, even as he dispensed absolution. I also knew he'd have to find a way to pay for it, and in the time it took to do so, I could perhaps make sure that Tolliver's check was made to Ike Enheer & Associates.

I didn't look up when Tolliver and the bureaucrat came out from the office. I finished painting the floor moldings, then took my brushes outside to the faucet to rinse them, nodding to Archibald Thacker, who was hauling out stuff that had been stored in the furnace room. I returned to the bus station and typed out a letter to Eldon Rubicoff telling him to please find out who owned the piece of property the highway guy had just described, and added that I'd see him in a week.

I'll admit that doing Tolliver dirty put a little spring in my step. It's true what they say about revenge being a dish best eaten cold.

"First he tells me he's a poor schlemiel who lives in a bus station, and now I find out he's an investor?" Rubicoff said. "Sophie, what do I do with this man?"

"You start padding his fee, like you do with that friend of your mother's cousin, Mr. I-Have-a-Chain-of-Jewelry-Stores,"

Sophie said, bracelets jangling on her wrists as she set a cup of coffee in front of me. She patted my hand. "Don't worry, I'm just kidding. I type all his bills. He charges what I tell him to charge."

Rubicoff gave her a baleful look. "I do not pad fees. There is an adjustable rate for well-heeled clients, which I alone invoke. Now, my quiet friend," he said, turning his attention back to me, "tell me what's going on. Why do you wish to buy this small patch of land in the country?"

I knew he would ask, so I'd already written an explanation. It was mostly fact—that I'd finally moved my money out of the shoeboxes and into stocks, but was interested in diversifying my portfolio (a useful phrase which, along with the aforementioned "discretionary account," I'd picked up by reading the financial press)—but pure fiction when it came to explaining why I'd settled on this property: some rubbish about my yearning for land, the need to work the soil, the feel of the good earth under my nails, heard it might be available at a good price, etc. I pulled the explanation from my coat pocket and pushed it across the desk. He took it, settled a pair of half-glasses low on his nose, and read it.

He finished with a sigh. "Sophie, it's clear our client believes it's best that we not know certain things."

"A good lawyer revels in his ignorance," she said. "Who told me that once?"

"What I meant was that you never ask your client if he's guilty of the crime he's charged with. I don't think our friend Mr. Ayers is committing a crime. You're not a criminal, are you?" he asked, turning to face me. I shook my head.

"See? It's no crime to buy land. It's no crime to buy it from a shell company. It's no crime for that company to have the same local address as one of my fellow members of the bar. And it's no crime for that lawyer to make a nice living by acting

177

as a front man for companies that wish to do their business privately. So let us not be suspicious, Sophie. Let us be merely curious."

"OK, I'm curious," she said. "Suspiciously curious."

Rubicoff picked up the paper I'd written and scanned it again. Sophie bustled about straightening things that didn't need straightening and brushing imaginary bits of dust from desktops and tabletops. Finally, he spoke again.

"But I must tell you, my loyal assistant, that I feel uneasy about this transaction."

"You worry too much," Sophie said. "And who says I'm your assistant? The only one doing any assisting around here is you, by signing everything I've already done."

"Indeed that's true. So perhaps I could assist you as you figure out why, when I called the office of my fellow attorney to ask about the property, he was expecting my call."

"Maybe he took some Dale Carnegie course where they told him to never act surprised, even when he is."

Rubicoff shrugged, then went on. "He didn't say, 'Why yes, Mr. Rubicoff, I've been expecting your call.' It was instead a lack of surprise. If someone called me out of the blue and said, 'Sir, I'd like to talk to you about buying your house,' I'd say, 'Are you sure you have the right house? Mine's not for sale.' And if this person said he indeed had the right house, it's that modest bungalow in Virginia Heights that needs a little paint and the front porch replaced, which I could do if I were a little better with a hammer, I'd say, 'What makes you think it's for sale?' But he didn't say that. When I got him on the phone and told him I represented a client that was interested in negotiating for a piece of property in Soque County registered under his name, you know what he said?"

"What?" Sophie asked.

"He said, 'Yes?'"

"That's all? Just 'Yes?'"

"That's all. He wasn't surprised or curious or puzzled. He didn't need a moment to remember exactly which property I was talking about. It was as if he had the file on the desk in front of him and had been told to expect a call."

Rubicoff shifted in his seat and settled back again. "But it gets even stranger. It turns out he wasn't expecting me to call after all. He was waiting for a call from someone else."

Even though he was talking to Sophie, Rubicoff watched me closely the whole time, speaking distinctly to make sure I understood. He paused at several points, which I took as my cue to jump in and scribble something down in explanation. But I sat impassively, keeping my face neutral. I was as mystified as he was.

"He wanted to know who my client was. Of course I refused to tell him. He knew I wouldn't, no more than he would tell me who the property owner is. Then he asked me to tell him a bit about my client. So I told him I was calling on behalf of a small, established investment firm whose activities had received some attention in the press in recent years. I told him the firm had a limited number of partners, invested in carefully selected opportunities, and preferred to keep a low profile. This is when he started sounding confused."

"No wonder," Sophie said. "I'm confused myself. This big-deal investment firm is our Mr. Ayers?"

"Just because he hasn't invested in anything yet—"

"Nothing but your legal bills," Sophie interrupted.

"—doesn't mean he's not an investor. That's what he's here to do now, isn't it?" he said, looking at me. I nodded.

"Anyway, the lawyer suddenly says he may have confused my client with someone else, and would I please describe for him again which property we're talking about. After I do so, he puts me on hold for several minutes, then comes back to say

179

he'll have to call me back. What does that sound like to you?"

"That he had somebody more important to talk to?" Sophie said helpfully.

"It sounds like to me that he'd been told to expect a call on the property from a certain party, and assumed that I was that party. When he figured out I wasn't, he put me on hold and tried to call whoever the real owner of the property is to ask what was going on. When he couldn't get him, he bought himself some time by saying he'd call me back. Which he did, just this morning."

Rubicoff finished with a flourish. "It seems that the law firm of Barton, Greer, and Pitts has a policy about negotiations for property sales: they must be done in person, with the buyer present. They want to meet you, my friend."

We had an appointment for the following week. I met Rubicoff at his office, and we went over together in a cab. Barton, Greer, and Pitts occupied two floors of a ten-story building in midtown Atlanta, just off Peachtree Street. We stepped off the elevator directly into a lavish reception area, with hardwood floors, Persian carpets, and two groups of chairs and couches set around low tables. In between them was a simple, elegant desk containing a telephone and lamp, with a severe-looking woman sitting primly behind it, legs crossed at the ankle, eyeing us as we strode toward her.

"May I help you?" she said, not sounding like she meant it.

"We're here to see Mr. Greer," Rubicoff said, handing her his business card. She held it by one corner, as if it were infectious.

"Is he expecting you?" she asked.

"He is," Rubicoff said.

"And your name, sir?" she said to me, coming down hard

on the "your" to make sure I understood that she knew this was all a joke of some kind. I'd considered buying a suit, but Rubicoff had dissuaded me, saying that I had a choice between looking like a pretender or an eccentric, and that the latter—having the advantage of being true—was more believable. So I stood there in my Salvation Army–issue clothes, trying to make the eccentricity ooze out of me while Rubicoff jumped in.

"His name is Mr. Ayers. Mr. Greer is expecting both of us."

She waved us over to one of the groups of chairs and picked up the phone. I started to sit down, but Rubicoff caught my arm and hauled me up, shaking his head. Instead, he maneuvered us to the side of the receptionist's desk, where he stood ostentatiously, with his coat open and his hands in his pockets, the very picture of an important man whose patience is being tested. After we spent a few minutes gazing at the ceiling and hovering over the receptionist, she picked up the phone a second time and murmured into it. A moment later, another woman came bustling up the corridor, walked over to us, and said, "Mr. Greer will see you now."

She led us to an office and showed us in. A bald, portly man wearing a bow tie and baggy tweed trousers held up with suspenders stood up behind his desk and extended his hand. "Mr. Rubicoff? I'm Carter Greer."

They shook hands; then Rubicoff gestured to me and said, "This is Samuel Ayers, who is the managing partner of the investment firm that's interested in purchasing your property." The lawyer gave me a hearty handshake as well, told us to sit, and settled into his chair. Over his shoulder, a large window offered a fabulous view of the Atlanta skyline.

For a moment, no one said anything as both Rubicoff and Greer waited for the other to begin. Finally, Rubicoff spoke up.

"I must say, sir, that this process is a bit irregular. Mr. Ayers is an intensely private man who has always preferred to manage his investments quietly. He's deaf, and as you may guess from his appearance, a bit unconventional in his approach to business. Perhaps you could explain why it was necessary to have him come here."

"I hope to do so, in due time," Greer said. "But as long as explanations are in order, I'm curious as to why your client decided on this property as the focus of his investment plans."

"I wasn't aware that one had to put up a reason along with the purchase price," Rubicoff said.

Greer looked exasperated. "Sir, please understand our position. The property wasn't advertised for sale. We haven't solicited a buyer. So when someone develops a sudden interest in it, it's only natural for us to want to know why."

Before Rubicoff could answer, the office door behind us opened a crack and a voice asked, "Ready, sir?"

"Yes, come in," Greer said. "Gentlemen, I took the liberty of ordering coffee." I shifted in my seat, following his gaze, and saw a black man wearing a white coat back into the room, holding a large silver tray in both hands and pushing the door open with his butt. When he turned around to look for a place to set the coffee, I saw his face. It was Archibald Thacker.

We stared at each other for a moment. Then he set the coffee tray on the edge of the desk and said to Greer, "I believe I need a few minutes alone with Sammy."

There are some things in life you're not sure you're seeing, even when you see them. Watching an important white lawyer be willingly ushered out of his own office by a black garbage hauler wearing servant's garb is one of them.

Greer stood up without hesitating and headed for the door. Rubicoff was rooted to his chair, confused by what had happened. When Greer reached the door, he stopped and said,

"Sir, since these two gentlemen apparently know each other, I suspect we're no longer needed."

Rubicoff got up slowly, swiveling his stare between Archibald and me. "I don't know what's going on here," he said, "but don't sign anything without talking to me first." Then, suddenly, both of them were gone with the door whispering shut behind them, and Archibald was sitting behind the lawyer's desk, just as comfortable as you please.

"Might as well have some coffee, since it's here," he said, pouring two cups and pushing one of them toward me. He lifted the lid on the sugar bowl and cursed. "Shit. Ain't but one lump in there. Can't find good help anywhere these days."

He settled back and regarded me over the rim of his cup. I felt like I'd just been caught doing something wrong and was waiting for judgment to be handed down. But then, Archibald himself had something to explain—like what the devil he was doing in this lawyer's office acting like the lord of the manor but pretending to be hired help. So I figured I would just brazen it out, cocking an eyebrow and giving him a so-what? look.

"You heard it, didn't you?" Archibald finally asked. "You heard them talking about the highway. Here I've been waiting for Tolliver to come sniffing around, and when the call comes, it ain't Tolliver at all. It's some lawyer nobody ever heard of claiming to represent some investment firm he won't name. So I tell Greer to get 'em in here, let me take a look. And I find you."

He took another sip of coffee, then set the cup on the desk.

"I saw you at the church that day. You were kneeling on the floor outside Tolliver's office, working on the trim or something. I was hauling stuff out of the furnace room. Awfulest mess you ever saw. Junk been thrown down there for years. Tolliver calls one day, says to haul it all away, and when I get there, I hear every word from his office, coming through the heating vent or something. The minute that old boy told Tolliver about the highway, I knew I'd hear from him. 'Cause I own all that land."

He said it for effect, and waited for me to react. I just sat.

"Look, I ain't gonna tell anybody anything. If you want to pretend to be deaf, that's your business. I don't understand why someone would want to live in a bus station all their life, doing shit work for white folks when they don't have to—" He stopped for a moment while a grin crossed his face. "See there? I'm talking about you like you're a nigger. Which is what everybody thinks. It would surely come as news that you ain't deaf and dumb after all."

Archibald shook his head. "Good God, man. You've been at this for, what, thirty years now? Barrington's own legend. You just appear one day, get off a bus, nobody knows who you are or where you come from. That soft-hearted fool Jenkins lets you hang around, and pretty soon you're here permanent. How come you never left? Once you got grown, you could have moved away, talked, and had a normal life."

I shrugged. Most of the normal lives I'd seen looked pretty wretched. My silence was my protection, and it helped me engage the world on my own terms. I'd have to be a fool to give that up to become just another yahoo yakking his way through life. But try to explain that to the tongue waggers.

"I always thought you were too smart for a dummy. Folks never had a problem making you understand anything. Now I know why. But look here. We both know something about each other now. I know you ain't a dummy, and you know that I ain't just a garbage hauler. Or at least I guess you know, considering what's happened here today. I've got a bunch of questions, and I'll bet you do too. Are you gonna talk to me?"

I shook my head.

"I didn't think so. Do you still want to buy that property?"

I hesitated. I couldn't imagine why he would consider selling it when he knew what I knew: that the state's highway plans would make that land highly valuable in a few years. But what the hell—he asked. I nodded.

"Well, I ain't interested in selling. At least to you," he said. "You've probably never been out there, taken a good look around, have you?"

I shook my head.

"Ain't nobody gonna build anything out there. There's at least four natural springs keeping the ground all wet and spongy. They may run the highway close by, but as soon as some state engineer gets out there and sees what the ground's like, they'll change their mind about putting an interchange there."

Archibald fell quiet, and seemed to be lost in thought. In the silence I could hear the ticking of the lawyer's clock, one of those tricky brass captain's clocks you wind with a big key and which have annoying, tinny chimes that are supposed to make you feel like a salty dog when you hear them. Finally, he spoke up.

"I was born out there, you know. Little old shacky place, gone now, off behind Snell's Mill in the woods. When I started getting some money a few years back, I bought the whole area. Don't know why. Sentimental, I guess. You can't do much with it, it's pretty much timbered out. I walked out there one time, you can't even tell where the house was anymore. I used to think it was important to own it. A symbol of some kind. I know now there are better symbols." He gave a sly grin. "Like having an important white lawyer handle your affairs for you."

Almost on cue, there came a tapping at the door and Greer came in. "Arch, let me tell you something out here," he said.

Archibald went into the corridor, where I heard them

muttering for a few moments. When he came back in, he said, "Well, what do you know. It seems we have someone else who wants to enter the bidding."

Archibald and I spent another hour in that office, me listening to him talk and nodding agreeably every once in a while as my contribution to the conversation. Given the chance, Tolliver probably would paint it as a session in which a pair of sharpies set out to bring his ruin. But it wasn't that organized. It started with Archibald asking casually, "Well, should we sell him the property?" and ended with the idea that with the exchange of a few simple letters, we could not only make Tolliver believe he had a chance to get the property, but make him pay dearly for the right to be the buyer.

The tale is again best picked up here by Percy Queen, insurance agent, co-conspirator, and snitch, told under oath in Soque circuit court in the trial of *Georgia* v. *Tynan:*

PROSECUTOR: How did you and Mr. Tynan identify the owner of the property?

PERCY: It was a bit tougher than we thought it'd be. I spent a couple of hours at the courthouse in the register-of-deeds office, had those big damn books open all over the place. Ain't no addresses out there where this land is, so you have to go strictly by the legal description. And if you ain't got the legal description, then you have to go to those books that got them maps in them and figure it out. Then once you have the legal description figured out, there's another book that records all the transfers of deeds. That's where we found the owner's name. I'll tell you, it's a damn sight easier when someone just puts up a For Sale sign with a phone number on it. [Laughter.]

PROSECUTOR: So Mr. Tynan did not participate in any of this research?

PERCY: No sir. He kept reminding me that he'd gotten the information on where the road was to be built, and that I should do the heavy lifting to even things up.

PROSECUTOR: But he was aware that you were doing this?

PERCY: You bet he was. He'd called three times before I got back to the office that afternoon.

PROSECUTOR: Did you identify the owner?

PERCY: Yes sir.

PROSECUTOR: And who was it?

PERCY: A lawyer in Atlanta. He actually described himself as a trustee, but said he had the legal power to make all decisions about the property.

PROSECUTOR: Did you identify yourself when you talked to this owner?

PERCY: I surely did.

PROSECUTOR: Did you mention Mr. Tynan's name at any point?

PERCY: I surely did, almost first thing. I told him that Tolliver was a prominent minister, and that I was a prominent businessman, and that we were interested in buying his property.

PROSECUTOR: And what did he say?

PERCY: He talked some lawyer talk about how he hadn't really considered putting it on the market, but he finally said he would consider selling a right of first refusal while he entertained an offer. Those were his exact words. Entertain an offer.

PROSECUTOR: Would you please explain to the court, Mr. Queen, what a right of first refusal is.

PERCY: Well, I actually had to have him explain it to me. He said that if we paid him a certain amount of money per acre, we would then get first crack at it if he decided to sell. And if we didn't like the price or something, he could then sell it to whoever he wanted. But in any event, we would be first in line.

PROSECUTOR: How long would this right of first refusal be good for?

PERCY: One year.

PROSECUTOR: How much did the property owner want you to pay for this right?

PERCY: Ten dollars an acre.

PROSECUTOR: How much property was involved?

PERCY: It was 182 acres, I believe.

PROSECUTOR: Was a price set? I mean, did the property owner tell you what the price would be if he ever decided to sell?

PERCY: No sir.

PROSECUTOR: Let me make sure I understand. The owner of
              the property wanted you to pay over eighteen
              hundred dollars for nothing more than the
              right to be first in line to pay some undeter-
              mined price for this land, even though he
              clearly had said he wasn't even sure he wanted
              to sell it?

PERCY: That's correct.

PROSECUTOR: And this was acceptable to you?

PERCY: Well, I didn't much care for it, but Tolliver
              was hot to do it.

PROSECUTOR: So did the two of you pay the ten dollars an
              acre for this right of first refusal?

PERCY: No sir.

PROSECUTOR: And why not?

PERCY: Well, by the time I got back to that lawyer,
              someone else had gotten into the bidding. It
              eventually cost us eighteen dollars an acre.

15

I'll say this: The film shot by the CBS crew the evening of the bonfire certainly made for dramatic television. I saw it again recently, as part of a reminiscence of the whole affair broadcast by an Atlanta TV station, and it truly is a remarkable bit of cinema. The camera was steady, the images were in focus, and the sound was clear; but at several points, the cameraman was jostled in the panic, or he made a quick pan to capture some fleeting moment of drama, so the film had that unmistakable immediacy of a real disaster in the making. And because he was standing on the flatbed trailer, with his feet at shoulder level to the crowd, the cameraman had an omniscient sweep of the grounds.

The drama begins with a woman screaming off-camera, "Oh my God, the church!" You hear a general hubbub breaking out, even as the camera stays focused on the record burners and the bonfire. Then you hear a second off-camera voice, a man this time, shouting, "Fire! FIRE!" and—if the station broadcasting the film has any balls and doesn't bleep it out—you hear CBS News correspondent Neal McNeal say, "Holy shit." Only then does the camera pan over to the church and you see it.

At first, it's just a glow from the windows, a church lit up on a summer Sunday evening, waiting for the congregation to gather. Then you notice the light has a life of its own, an arrhythmic undulation that seems to swell behind the glass. Then two windows explode and flames come roaring out, reaching for the eaves and roof. There is the sound of screaming and shouted, unintelligible instructions, and in the gloom of the foreground you see several figures running near the church, desperate to do something but repelled by the heat. There is a faint clanging in the distance, which Barrington residents recognize as the alarm at the main fire station going off. Another window explodes, this one like the first two near the pulpit end of the church, and the extra oxygen gives the flames more vigor. Someone rushing to get off the flatbed trailer bumps into the cameraman, and there is a second or two of blurry, impressionistic images of the steeple set against a sky gone almost completely dark, sidelit by the flickering fire. Almost everyone is shouting or screaming now, and you see more people moving in the foreground, unable to do anything but unwilling to be still. A piece of burning material of some kind floats down, and a man does a strange dance around it as he stomps it out.

Then, out of the confusion rings a voice so clearly full of stress and horror that it becomes the insistent focus of attention even as the camera keeps trained on the church. "You did this!" the voice shouts, accusatory and menacing. "Do you know what this means?"

The camera pans away from the church, inexorably drawn to the voice. It searches for a moment, the cameraman obviously unsure whose voice it is, until you hear it again, even louder this time: "DO YOU KNOW WHAT THIS

191

MEANS?" The camera finds the shouter. It is Tolliver, hair disheveled and eyes full of fury, leaning into Perry Ray Pruitt's face. Around them, people have fallen back a step, pushed away by Tolliver's apparent rage. The camera looks down on Tolliver and Perry Ray, close enough to them as they stand near the flatbed trailer so that they dominate the frame. They are turned toward the church and the flames highlight one side of their faces. But because the camera is over Perry Ray's shoulder, only Tolliver's face is fully visible, and the combination of his anger and the sidelighting that leaves half his face in shadow gives him a particularly demonic cast. For a second or two, nothing happens, but the camera is riveted while the shouting and crackling goes on in the background.

Then Tolliver raises his arm, so suddenly that you see Perry Ray flinch, and points to the church. "You started this," he says, his voice barely under control. "Now make it stop."

Perry Ray turns toward the church, and the camera edges away slightly, to get a better angle on the two of them. Tolliver's arm is still raised, and for a moment the two are motionless. Then Tolliver draws his arm back and jabs it at the church again, and shouts, "MAKE IT STOP!"

Perry Ray moves so quickly the camera is caught by surprise, leaving you looking at Tolliver on one side of the frame, with the space formerly filled by Perry Ray suddenly empty. The camera swings around toward the church again, just in time to see Perry Ray push his way through the crowd and hesitate at its edge. Then, with screams of horror trailing behind him, he runs straight into the church, going in the front door and yanking it open just as one of the roof beams apparently falls inside. You see Perry Ray draw back with his forearm over his eyes as the rush of hot air is drawn out by the open door, then he plunges inside despite cries and shouts of "No, no!" The cameraman is again jostled as two other figures run toward the door and are driven back by the heat. Something else falls inside, and suddenly the roof is open and sparks and flames are pouring out of the top of the church. In the background, a fire engine blasts its horn as it pulls up close. Then, miraculously, Perry Ray appears in the doorway, silhouetted by the flames. He stops, leans one hand against the doorframe and stands, seeming to pant. He then collapses. A fireman, wearing a long coat with "BFD" written in large yellow letters across the back, runs up to the door and squats down, lifts Perry Ray over his shoulder like a sack of grain, and turns to bring him back.

Had Perry Ray been a bit lighter, or the fireman a bit quicker, they'd have made it. But even as the fireman bends down, you see a beam in the roof above the church's high porch begin to sag. Just as the fireman begins his turn, it drops. On the film, it seems to just brush by Perry Ray's head, but its skull-crushing force knocks both of them to the ground. A curtain of sparks is raised, but behind them you see the fireman struggle to his feet as another fireman runs up. Together, with a hand under each armpit, they drag Perry Ray into the yard, away from the flames.

Until then, the cameraman had been rooted to his spot on the flatbed trailer, his movement limited to panning the camera. But with Perry Ray on the ground, the cameraman apparently decides on a close-up. You hear his disembodied voice say, "C'mon, we're moving," to the soundman, and the film begins moving jerkily as he runs. A few dozen faces, captured in blurry half-second capsules as he shoulders his way through the crowd, become a frieze of horror. When the camera finds Perry Ray, his rescuers and other onlookers have already bowed to the obvious and withdrawn a few steps. The camera stops at Perry Ray's feet; beyond his head is the church, still blazing.

At this point, the cameraman does a simple, remarkable thing. In an instinctive effort to find the best frame for the image he sees through the camera's viewfinder, he moves himself to the right of Perry Ray's feet and slowly sinks to his knees. Then for about ten seconds, until the end of the film, he stays perfectly still, the only movement coming from the dance of the flames in the background.

It was this image that fixed itself permanently in America's mind, thanks to countless replayings of the film and to the *Life* magazine cover taken from it. Perry Ray's body is in the foreground, head lolled over to one side and arms flung out, a Christ-like pose on the lawn. Behind him, the church is fully engulfed, with flames at every window and the steeple showing as only a rigid shadow in a fire-brightened sky. And just off to the side of Perry Ray's head is a record album cover that somehow escaped the fire and was dropped in the panic. John Lennon's face was clearly visible below its title:

Meet the Beatles!

16

I'd done everything exactly as Archibald suggested. I drafted a letter on Ike Enheer & Associates stationery offering twelve dollars per acre for the right of first refusal on the property, keeping a copy for my file. When the letter from Arch's lawyer came back—saying an offer of fourteen dollars per acre had been received, and did we wish to submit a new proposal?—I stapled the envelope to the letter, thus keeping the postmark as proof of delivery date, and placed it in the file as well. We then repeated this exercise with a second set of letters, with me offering sixteen dollars and getting a letter back saying the competing bid was now up to eighteen. I bowed out at that point with a thanks-but-no-thanks letter.

"We'll stop after two bumps in the price," Archibald had said that day in his lawyer's office, when we cooked up the plan. "We don't want to be greedy about this, and we'll need to leave a paper trail in case anyone comes around later on. Just keep everything Greer sends you."

Arch had one other piece of advice: Keep Rubicoff in the dark.

G. D. Gearino

"Don't tell him any of this. Make him think you really want the property," he said. "Let him make the offers and answer the letters. Don't ever get in a spot where you need a lawyer to lie for you. Most of them will give you up in a second."

Ironically, I never got a dime out of it. Arch said we'd split whatever Tolliver could be made to pay, but I never saw it. To be fair, I couldn't really claim an interest in the deal; it was Arch's land to do with as he saw fit. The only thing I invested was a pair of letters written only to drive the price up. But in the end, it cost me several hundred dollars in fees to Rubicoff, plus the price of a few bus tickets to Atlanta, and for all that I got squat.

At least Arch's advice was good, which I found out when the investigator visited after the fire. Good for him, at least.

Responding to that irresistible impulse to visit the scene of a tragedy, virtually everyone in Barrington drove or walked by the church the day after the fire. The cars crawled by as their occupants peered out, with some pulling over to the curb so that they could devote their full attention to gawking. Others gathered in clumps on the edge of the church lawn, beyond the yellow ribbon that wound between the sawhorses arson investigators had placed to keep the curious out of the ruins. Almost everyone had been there the night before, had seen the events unfold in person, and would watch them again that evening on CBS News, but still they pointed out to one another the spot to which Perry Ray's body had been dragged.

The church made an imposing wreck. Its roof was gone and all but one window had been blown out by the fire or smashed by fire fighters. Soot stains marked the brick above every opening, the plumes misshapen by the jets of water that had been directed into the church's interior but sometimes

196

found the wall instead. The massive Doric columns on the front were burned completely away, as were the wooden doors. Inside, you could see a charred roof beam propped where it had fallen against a wall. A smoky, wet smell pervaded.

I circled the perimeter of the church property, ignored as usual by everyone. I saw one of Archibald's garbage trucks at the far edge of the side parking lot, away from the lawn where the bonfire had been held. I found him standing under a tree by himself, hands in his pockets, staring at the church.

"I don't know who's the bigger son of a bitch," Arch said as I walked up. "You or Tolliver."

I knew then that he knew. He'd figured it out somehow as he stood there, and for a moment I was afraid he'd tell. Then I realized he couldn't finger me without explaining how a couple of hundred gallons of moonshine came to be stored in the church's baptismal font. Once again, we were bound by our mutual secrets.

"They'll figure it out, you know," he said. "A good arson investigator can tell all kinds of things about a fire. Hell, he can probably tell whether it was lit with a kitchen match or a Zippo."

Still facing the church, Arch nodded in its direction. "Somebody's gonna come over here and see the same thing I see. And when they do, things are gonna get real interesting. 'Cause when people die in fires that shouldn't have happened, other people get upset."

I stared at the church, and in a moment I saw it too. All around the outside of the building, the shrubs and grass had burned in a rough but consistent pattern. In one spot, however, at the door leading to the back of the church where Arch and his son had siphoned off the moonshine, there was a great tongue of burned grass spreading out from the building at least thirty-five feet. In the middle of that tongue was a long,

197

thin line of charred material, and at its end was the only clue an investigator would need: a brass coupling that clearly identified it as the remains of a garden hose.

"When I left yesterday, that was coiled up nice against the building. And we had the end sealed up good," Arch said. "Now this morning, I can see that somebody pulled that hose away from the building and unplugged the end." He withdrew his hand from his pocket. In it was a wadded mass of cloth and tape, redolent of moonshine.

I recognized it immediately. The night before, I'd ripped it from the end of the hose and tossed it away into the darkness.

"I don't care about losing the liquor. I'll just have to make good on it. And I don't care 'bout Tolliver's church. It'll get rebuilt. But maybe it wouldn't have burned if you hadn't poured that stuff all over the ground, leaving it to set there in a pool waiting for some spark to come floating down from that fire. And if it hadn't burned, that boy wouldn't have died."

Across the lawn a television camera crew was setting up, this one from an Atlanta television station. CBS, it seemed, no longer had a monopoly on the story. For a moment, Arch watched them, then turned his attention back to me.

"Do you really hate Tolliver that much? Or do you just hate everybody?" he asked. I shrugged.

He tossed me the plug and turned to go. Then, remembering something else, he stopped and faced me again.

"I don't know where all this will lead, but I'll tell you one thing. No one will ever believe you if you say some old nigger is hauling liquor. And if anyone ever comes around to ask about that property, you're on your own. My name's not connected to any company, and with what I pay that lawyer Greer, he'll take nails through the hand before he'll give me up."

Arch was a clever man. Through observation and intuition, he'd figured out what happened just by standing on the church lawn for a few minutes, mulling things over in his mind. He knew that moonshiners often test for proof by pouring a cupful of liquor on a fire; when it doesn't flame up anymore, they stop the run. In other words, it burns.

I wasn't as familiar with liquor making, so I wasn't sure. But I hadn't had time to research the question the night before, when I'd seen the chimney of sparks head into the sky. Fate had whispered in my ear, telling me to move quick because I'd never get a better chance to even up with Tolliver. "Just pour it out and see what happens," the whisper said.

Archibald walked to his truck, climbed into the cab, and drove away. Not long after, the hauling company was sold to a national waste firm and the Thacker population in Barrington began thinning out. I never saw him again.

The thing about cops is, you never know how much they know. I sat in Rubicoff's office, waiting as the investigator scratched a few notes on a pad—engaging in the classic cop technique of letting the tension build—and I tried to calculate what he knew.

There were certain things that everyone had heard. Two days after the fire, the *Barrington Chronicle* reported that its origin was being called "suspicious." The fire chief was quoted as saying that evidence suggested a massive amount of some flammable liquid had helped fuel the blaze. A week later, the *Chronicle* reported something else that had been whispered around town for several days: The church's insurance policy had lapsed before the fire.

The article said insurance officials wouldn't comment and that efforts to reach Tolliver had been unsuccessful. But it quoted an unnamed church deacon as saying that Tolliver and Percy Queen had appeared at a deacons' meeting to say that there had been some mix-up with the paperwork on the renewal of the policy, and that the insurer was claiming it wasn't legally bound to pay for rebuilding the church. The deacon told the *Chronicle* Percy had assured them that it was a routine dispute, that the payment had either been lost in the mail or misdirected at the home office. In any event, Percy had told the deacons, all policies carry a grace period in which they remain in force even if a payment hasn't yet been received, to protect policyholders from hardnose tactics in this very kind of happenstance.

But there had been no further word that the dispute was settled, and now here was this investigator in Rubicoff's office, focused on his notes and ignoring Sophie as she fluttered about asking if he didn't want some coffee and a bagel, she could run get one, and cream cheese, too, it wouldn't be a problem, really.

Finally, he spoke. "Mr. Rubicoff, have you explained to your client why we're here?"

"I've told him what you've told me—which isn't much," Rubicoff said. "But before you start, please understand that if I don't like the way this is going, I'll have to insist that you leave."

The investigator gave him a flat stare. "You don't need to explain your client's rights to me, sir. And I'd like for you to understand that I can have Mr. Ayers answer questions in a more formal setting if this session is a problem for him."

Rubicoff turned to me and said, "What our friendly neighborhood storm trooper is trying to say is, he'll drag you down to the grand jury if he doesn't like your answers." Shifting back to the investigator, he added, "My homeless, deaf, almost penniless client is ready to entertain your questions now."

I'd arrived an hour before the investigator, summoned by a telegram from Rubicoff two days earlier. The message had been cryptic but urgent: "Property purchase effort being probed by state officials. Need to be here Thursday 9 a.m. Reply if can't come. Important." When I got there, Rubicoff had every document he'd ever prepared for me or received on my behalf—incorporation papers, letters, and investment records—spread out before him. He tapped his finger on a pile of papers that I recognized as the exchange of letters about the property. "This will either hang you or help you," he said. "I don't know which. Is there any reason why I shouldn't show him these?"

I shook my head. On the bus ride to Atlanta that morning, I'd come to appreciate Archibald's wisdom. Who could have seen, six months prior when the whole chain of events was put into motion, that the church would burn down and a feckless loser like Perry Ray Pruitt would get his skull crushed? Archibald and I both knew Tolliver didn't have money; everyone knew that. We expected he would beg or borrow a few thousand dollars for the purchase rights. We didn't expect that he'd steal it. But Arch had a nose for the unexpected, and knew the deal would have to withstand scrutiny. Hence the letters. If anyone asks, he said, show them to 'em.

What I didn't realize until the inspector began posing his questions, however, was that there was only one butt covered.

"Mr. Ayers, your attorney tells me you have a remarkable ability to read lips, so I'll just plunge right in," he said. "Are you the principal owner of Ike Enheer and Associates?"

I nodded.

"Does anyone else have a financial interest in the firm?"

I shook my head.

"Would you please describe for me exactly what Ike Enheer and Associates does," he said, pushing a pencil and pad of paper across the desk to me.

I scribbled on the pad and pushed it back to him. He read

my answer: "It's a diversified investment company."

A flicker of annoyance crossed his face. "Do you have annual financial statements detailing the company's investments? And can I please see them?" he asked.

Rubicoff jumped in. "I thought we were going to talk about a specific negotiation for a specific bit of real estate. Why do you need to know Mr. Ayers's financial affairs?"

"Because I don't think Mr. Ayers has any financial affairs. I think his company is a sham."

"It's not against the law to run an unsuccessful company," Rubicoff said.

"But it is against the law to conspire to steal confidential government information," the investigator said.

"What are you talking about?" Rubicoff asked, genuinely puzzled. "He became interested in some property, he made two bids for the right to buy that property and finally gave up. That's the end of the story."

"No, that's the beginning of the story," the investigator said, suddenly animated. "I've got a church that's been burned down, an insurance company that says it's being defrauded, and a piece of swampland that everyone suddenly seems to want to buy. I've got a fancy-pants lawyer in Atlanta who won't say who actually owns the property, and his secretary treats me like I'm something stuck to the bottom of her shoe. I've got a dead preacher on the cover of *Life* magazine, and everyone from CBS News to the *New York Times* is poking around Barrington goddam Georgia asking questions. Now somebody's gonna tell me what was going on here, and your client can begin by explaining why the hell he wanted to buy that property."

Rubicoff, surprised by the sudden fury, said nothing. The investigator reached into his coat pocket and withdrew a folded paper, slapping it down on the desk.

"You're right, Mr. Rubicoff. I will drag your client's butt

down to the grand jury if I have to. Here's the subpoena. Tell him he has a choice. We can stay here, where you can hold his hand, or he and I can go to the grand jury hearing room to talk about this while you cool your heels outside." He shifted his gaze to me. "You don't get to have your lawyer hang around when you testify before the grand jury. And forget about your Fifth Amendment rights. You don't get to decline to answer questions. And you know what? In there, the district attorney's not nearly the restrained, polite soul I am here."

The investigator leaned back, crossed his arms over his chest, and waited. For a moment, the three of us sat perfectly still. Even Sophie, who normally could be counted on in tense moments to pat someone's arm and offer them a bite to eat, was quiet in the anteroom. Finally, Rubicoff spoke up.

"I'm sure there's a reasonable explanation for everything. If you'll give me a few minutes alone with my client, we can probably avoid a visit to your rubber-hose room."

*The laws are changed now, of course. Before a trial even begins, pros-*ecutors these days must reveal who they'll call as witnesses, and even make those witnesses available to defense attorneys for questioning. But back in 1966, prosecutors and police could still spring a surprise witness in a trial (as well as withhold evidence, search without warrants, and arrange for black suspects to slip in the jailhouse shower until they confessed—ah, those were the good old days, when justice was a terrible swift sword). So Tolliver didn't even know it was coming until the prosecutor boomed out, "The state calls Mr. Samuel Ayers."

I was sitting in the back of the courtroom, having been admitted during a break, so I rose and walked down the center aisle until I came to the rail behind the lawyers' tables. As the prosecutor swung open the gate for me, Tolliver shifted around to look. His face carried both a look of disbelief and a smirk. I let myself be led to the witness stand, placed my hand on the Bible, and listened as the bailiff asked if I swore to tell the truth, the whole truth, and nothing but the truth.

I have to confess that I lied at the very beginning of this tale. I said I'd never uttered a word since stepping off the bus on that early spring morning in 1940. It's not true. I uttered 10,133 words, all in one afternoon, according to the court transcript. Here were the first two:

"I do."

17

There's only one more thing to tell, and to do that I'll have to jump ahead twenty years. But first, let me tie up the loose ends.

Tolliver was convicted, of course, largely on the strength of my testimony. After I'd explained to the investigator in Rubicoff's office that day how Tolliver came into possession of the road plans, the case fell into place. Working back from the notes I scribbled out for him, the investigator identified which member of the highway department's land-acquisition staff had been fired for a chronic drinking problem, and discovered that certain papers were missing from the man's files when they were retrieved from storage. When the investigator learned that the man had been killed in a car accident, he tracked down the widow and borrowed a photograph to show me. In court, I identified the photo as the man I saw go into Tolliver's office one winter morning to change his fate, only to propel Tolliver into sealing his own. Then I told what I had heard.

Percy Queen did some damage too. He'd rolled over on

Tolliver almost immediately, striking a deal to save his own hide in return for his testimony. I supplied the motive for looting the church's insurance fund, while Percy supplied the detail on how it actually happened.

I don't know about Percy, but I certainly lied. Even though I had to come clean on my own effort to buy the property—the prosecutor, following smart courtroom procedure, brought it up in his own questioning, eliminating the chance that Tolliver's attorney could use it to discredit me—I denied knowing who the owner of the land was. And I embellished the conversation between Tolliver and the late highway department employee: I had them on their knees praying together in Tolliver's office that day, the man a picture of strength and virtue as he confronted his demons, Tolliver the very soul of deceit as he urged further confession and revelation. The poor man was a drunken fool with a wife who preferred the company of Holy Rollers; I figured I could restore some shred of honor to his name, and pile it on Tolliver at the same time.

The defense depended on two strategies. First, it sought to prove that I really was deaf, so I couldn't have heard the conversation that I alleged took place. Tolliver's attorney, apparently believing I was able to understand his questions only by watching his lips, had me turn around in the witness chair and face the wall during his cross-examination. After I answered several subsequent questions, he asked the judge if he could blindfold me as well.

"Would you like for me to gag him too?" asked the judge, with exasperation in his voice. I was allowed to turn around and face the courtroom again.

Second, the defense noted that the prosecution had failed to produce the highway plan allegedly given to Tolliver. The reason was obvious: It had burned up along with everything else in his office. Still, Tolliver's attorney kept making sarcastic

references to "the purported documents" and at one point
held up a clear plastic sandwich bag filled with ash and shook it
in front of the jury, saying, "Here is the state's evidence of
wrongdoing. This, ladies and gentlemen, is said to be stolen secrets."

It didn't work. After only a couple of hours of delibera-
tion, the jury came back with guilty verdicts in charges of
grand theft and attempted fraud. Tolliver was sentenced to
three years in prison, with two years suspended due to the fact
he was a first offender.

I suppose the torment of his lessers, the killing of a girlfriend, and the hounding of a young preacher to his grisly
death don't count as offenses. But even if the law couldn't even
up the score, I still had one more shot at it.

Ironically, I became deaf again after the trial. The moment I stepped
down from the witness chair, I reverted to my old ways: I went
back to the bus station, kept my mouth shut, and began sweeping or raking again whenever I was needed. After a while, the
stares and whispers trailed off and people treated me much as
they had before the trial. A town hates to give up its eccentrics.

Tolliver was allowed to serve his time in the Soque County
jail. The judge evidently concluded it would do no good to send
a soft white man to the state penitentiary in Reidsville, a brutal
place set in the flat landscape of south Georgia. I thought it was
a capital idea; making Tolliver spend a year as somebody's bitch
would have made me feel like there was a certain order in the
universe. But the judge didn't ask for my sentencing recom-
mendation. Tolliver was released after nine months and moved
to Atlanta, where he spent two decades as an heir-in-waiting.
Alford's will had called for control of his estate to be turned
over to his firstborn child upon the event of Maddie's death,

and I suppose Tolliver decided he could kill time in Atlanta more easily than he could kill time in Barrington.

Perry Ray Pruitt was buried two days after the fire, laid to rest in the Barrington Baptist Church cemetery. His father explained to reporters covering the service that the fire was clearly arson and likely was the work of Jehovah's Witnesses. "This church had the tallest steeple in Barrington, and now it's gone," he said ominously. "That should tell you something."

The church was never rebuilt. The deacons voted to sue the insurer to collect on the policy, but after Tolliver's indictment they saw it was a losing cause, and abandoned the idea. The ruins stood for another year until the city demanded that the site be cleaned up. The parishioners—most of whom held thousands of dollars' worth of Barrington Baptist bonds which had gone into default—understandably declined to pay this final tax on Tolliver's theft, so the city condemned the property, razed the ruins, and turned the site into a municipal parking lot. Guided by the distinctly American tendency toward big-scale names for small-scale history, it was christened the Pruitt Memorial Parking Facility.

The arson investigation remains officially unsolved, but I suppose they can close the books on it now. Rubicoff warned me that there's no statute of limitations on arson if a death is involved, but I don't care. There's no evidence against me beyond my own word, and I could impeach that in quick time: I'll claim that during my daily breakfast with Jesus, he told me to confess.

Percy Queen's agreement with prosecutors called for him to plead guilty to one count of conspiracy to commit fraud, for which he was placed on probation. He was forced by state regulators to sell his insurance agency, found work as a used-car salesman, was caught in an odometer-tampering sting a few years later, and fled the state. His whereabouts remain unknown to this day, although I can't be the only person who has noticed how much radio provocateur Rush Limbaugh resembles Percy. I've notified the authorities.

The Thackers eventually disappeared altogether. Among Barrington's white folks, only I noticed they were gone, until the early 1980s, when Arch's fortune became too large to hide and the financial press discovered him and rooted out his background. (Are Em Jones's public humiliation began shortly afterwards, when he walked into a downtown diner for breakfast one morning and someone called out, "Hey, Are Em, Jesse Jackson called. He needs you to run a few errands for him.") After a number of years in Chicago, Arch bought a home in Palm Beach, Florida, where he caused an uproar by having a junked car and the rusting carcass of a washing machine dragged to the edge of his estate, near the road where everyone could see. Outraged city officials demanded that the mess be removed, but Arch's lawyer refused, saying that the city obviously couldn't discern between junk and "environmental art." The last I heard, the whole thing was still being hashed out in court. Outside of Arch's family, I'm probably the only person who got the joke.

Lucille fell victim to her own grease. She developed a chronic heart problem and was forced to give up the lunch counter. She moved in with her sister over in Flowery Branch and died in 1971. I still have the Christmas card she sent one year, which said simply, "You will always be precious to me." Occasionally I make the bus trip to Flowery Branch to tidy up around her grave. It's what I do best; you can't expect much from me while you're alive, but the minute you die, I'm there with the clippers and weed digger. I may even tend to Tolliver's grave someday, during the breaks I take from dancing atop it.

Tallasee Tynan still lives in Barrington when she's not off somewhere taking photographs. About two years after the fire,

Life magazine published a twelve-page spread of photos she took at a hippie commune. I can't imagine how any woman, after seeing the pictures, could have considered joining up: in every photo that showed work being done, a woman was doing it, while in every photo that showed dope smoking or lounging going on, a man was doing it. The next year, Tallasee published a book of photographs of the hippies, which sent reviewers into a frenzy of phrase making as they praised her ability to capture the "didactic antimaterialism" or the "prairie movement–inspired cultural revanchism" of her subjects.

She once asked if she could take my picture, but I declined. I scribbled a note that said I preferred a family portrait. She didn't understand until later.

Maddie Tynan died April 26, 1986, and was laid to rest next to Alford in the spot that had awaited her for almost fifty years. Three weeks after the funeral, Rubicoff arrived at the bus station at the appointed time. I was waiting for him outside, sitting on the same bench I'd claimed that morning so long ago. Beside me was the modest suitcase my mother had packed.

"Are you ready?" Rubicoff asked. I nodded.

"Is everything in there?" he said, tilting his head toward the suitcase. I nodded again. We set off for the lawyer's office.

I'd filled Rubicoff in some years before, so he was prepared to act when Maddie died. An uncontested and carefully crafted will like Alford's normally wouldn't have landed in probate court. But because state law requires estates of a certain size to be handled under the court's supervision, an administrator had been appointed. Rubicoff had arranged a meeting with him, taking care to explain that no challenge of the will was anticipated. Instead, Rubicoff said, his client had some important papers belonging to the estate and he merely wanted to present them. I carried them in the suitcase.

The administrator evidently had notified Tolliver and Tallasee of the meeting, because both were in his office waiting room when we arrived. It was the first time I'd seen Tolliver since the trial twenty years before; he hadn't made it a point to look me up on his rare visits from Atlanta.

There were no greetings. "What was that business with the radio?" he said roughly as we entered. "The guard says every inmate can have a radio and he hands me a package from you. And what do I find? A busted old piece of crap with all the pieces rattling around inside. I was supposed to listen to that?"

I was disappointed that he hadn't recognized it. But I just smiled, which seemed to infuriate him.

"Answer me, you fraudulent fart. God knows you can be quite the chatterbox when you want to."

Tolliver hadn't worn his exile well. He'd affected a hip, mid-1980s look—meaning a ponytail and permanent three-day beard—but instead of the casually sinister appearance he wanted, he merely seemed seedy. His hair was lank and thin, and the stubble was a gray ash smudged across his cheeks and chin. The cuffs of his sport coat were frayed and a button was missing from the right sleeve. When he stepped close, seeming to want to shake an answer out of me, I smelled the sweet, fermented breath of a dedicated drinker.

Just then, the administrator came out of his office and moved toward us. "Are you Mr. Rubicoff?" he said, reaching out to shake hands. "I recognize Sammy there. Why don't you come in and tell me what this is about." He herded us into his office, stopping at the threshold to say to Tolliver and Tallasee, "Give us a few minutes, then we'll all talk."

It was more than a few minutes. In the two hours we were in his office, the expression on the administrator's face went from polite interest to puzzlement, disbelief, wonderment, and finally, resignation. When Rubicoff had answered the last of his questions, he pushed away from his desk and stood. "We've

211

got to bring them in and tell them," he said, not seeming to look forward to the task.

Tolliver and Tallasee trooped in at his invitation. After circling back around behind his desk and sitting, the administrator opened his mouth to speak, but Tolliver cut him off.

"What the devil is going on here? What business can this idiot"—he jerked his head in my direction, lest someone be confused about which idiot he meant—"possibly have with us?"

Again, the administrator began to speak, but this time it was Rubicoff who interrupted.

"This idiot is Alford Tynan's son," he said. "Try to speak kindly of your brother."

At the administrator's invitation, Rubicoff set it out for them.

"A long time ago, back in the mid-1920s, a young woman named Lillian Ayers went to work in your father's law office. It isn't clear where she came from, or what her background was, but she was an attractive and lively young woman. She apparently caught your father's eye, and the two of them had an affair."

"How do you know these things?" Tolliver asked, challenge in his voice.

"Most of what I'll tell you is provable and documented. We had a private detective track the whereabouts of the people who worked in the office. Most are dead, but we found a secretary who provided us with an affidavit. She's elderly now, but her memory is quite clear. And we found the payroll records and check ledgers from your father's law firm in storage at the firm that inherited his clients.

"But let me move on with the story. Lillian became pregnant as a result of the affair. In order to avoid a scandal, she was sent to live in Birmingham, Alabama, where Sammy was born. I suspect you didn't know this," Rubicoff said to Tolliver, "but you and Sammy were born on the same day.

"It's not clear why Lillian was sent to Birmingham. We haven't found any family in the area—in fact, we haven't found any family at all. It's likely that Alford chose Birmingham because it was far enough away to discourage her from making impulsive visits back to Barrington, which she could have easily done from Atlanta. Also, it seems that Alford was friends with a partner at a Birmingham law firm, and this is how money was given to Lillian. Records from Alford's firm show a regular payment to the Birmingham firm. Unfortunately, that firm's files from the time don't exist anymore, but we found the partner. He also has provided an affidavit. It's couched in discreet lawyerly phrases, and he obviously still feels some loyalty to his old friend Alford, but it's clear that the firm was a conduit for child support payments to Lillian.

"Interestingly, the old lawyer helped fill out Lillian's background a bit. He visited her once after Alford asked him to look in on her. They evidently talked for a while. Like everyone else, he remembers her as a pretty young woman. But he also thought that whatever thin veneer of sophistication she'd developed by working with Alford had already started to erode. He described her as crude, with a sharecropper accent that crept into her speech. And while she obviously loved her baby, he noticed that her attention to it was a bit haphazard, even in the short time he was there.

"So if I had to make a guess—and a guess is the only thing we're likely to ever have—I would say that Lillian had simply walked away from some hardscrabble farm somewhere and found her way to Barrington. She was pretty enough to make men want to help her, and shrewd enough to take advantage of that."

Rubicoff paused, as if inviting a question. When none came, he continued.

"Anyway, she lived in Birmingham for ten years, with the checks coming regularly each month. Then one day, in 1940,

213

the check didn't show up. What happened between that moment and the day Sammy arrived in Barrington is mostly conjecture. He remembers a little of it, and some nosing around has helped fill in the blanks. But frankly, it's guesswork.

"When it was clear the check wasn't coming, Lillian likely called the Birmingham law firm. When no one there was able to help her, she probably called Alford's law office. It was then that she learned he was dead.

"She had come to depend on support from Alford. And even if she could have found a job somewhere, it wasn't exactly a time that accommodated the needs of working mothers. But she still must have had the courage and fearlessness that helped her walk away from a godforsaken farm years before. She packed a few things in a suitcase, tacked a note on the door of her apartment saying she'd be back in a few days, and headed for the bus station with Sammy. In all likelihood, she was headed for Barrington to make a claim on his behalf to Alford's estate.

"It was a long, overnight bus trip, with a number of stops along the way. During a particularly long stop in Anniston, Alabama, Lillian decided to stretch her legs. She was restless, Sammy was sound asleep in his seat, and there was a lively joint across the street. So she popped in for a few minutes. She was still a well-practiced flirt, so it was only moments before a young soldier offered to buy her a drink. They chatted happily for a few minutes until Lillian decided it was time to get back to the bus. The soldier was already drunk, and he became angry when she made to leave. He followed her out of the joint, pulled her into the shadows, and raped and killed her. This all took place not thirty yards from her sleeping son.

"The bus left without her, and Sammy slept soundly through the night. When he awoke, he was in Barrington. Alone, confused and scared."

Rubicoff again paused for a moment. Tallasee's eyes were glistening and even Tolliver had dropped his defiant, screw-you expression. Of course, I knew where all this was going, so I had to concentrate on not looking smug.

"You know this part of the story, so we can skip over it. He stayed here, he grew up here, he'll probably die here. But I'll tell you how Sammy came to discover that Alford Tynan was his father.

"Do you remember Jenkins, the bus station manager? I know you've heard the story of how he looked after Sammy. I didn't know him, of course, but by all accounts he was a friendly fellow. He was also a man with a secret. At some point, he evidently looked through the suitcase Sammy's mother left behind. He probably assumed it was lost luggage and hoped to find a clue as to its owner. Well, he found a clue, all right. What he found was proof that Alford was Sammy's father.

"So you know what he did with this proof? He pushed it away in a storage locker and left it there for almost twenty years. It's anyone's guess why. He was a lonely man and Sammy was the closest thing to family he had. Perhaps he also thought, in an odd way, that he was protecting Sammy from something. And protecting others. He probably just didn't see what good would come of it.

"But when he died, Sammy got the key to the storage locker and discovered the suitcase. And what he found out about his father made him want to find out what happened to his mother.

"Between his memory of the trip and highway maps from the time, he was able to deduce the likely route taken by the bus the night his mother disappeared. He then began visiting the towns along the route, one by one. He would go to the local library, find the newspapers for the period and search them for clues. In Anniston, he found the story of the murder. The date

215

matches, the location matches, even the description of the mur-
dered woman's clothes matches Sammy's memory of what she
wore that night. He found her grave in the city cemetery. It was
marked by a modest tombstone which, of course, carried no
name. He decided to have a proper marker carved for the grave.
But he realized he didn't even know her full name or birthday.

"He knew where he could find out, though. When he arrived back in Barrington, he pulled the suitcase down from the
storeroom shelf where he'd hidden it. I'd like to show you the
two pieces of paper that suitcase contained.

"First is this sheet of letterhead from Alford's law firm,
with a handwritten note scribbled to Lillian. It says simply that
if she has an emergency to call him. There's a phone number
on it, written old-style, with letters as well as numbers. I'm
sure you'll recognize it. Mrs. Tynan had the same phone number her whole life." Rubicoff passed around a photocopy of the
note.

"We had a handwriting expert examine the note, by the
way. It's his considered opinion that Alford wrote it.

"But the more important paper is this birth certificate."
Again, Rubicoff handed out a copy. "It matches perfectly with
the original filed in the state archive in Montgomery. As you
can see, the father is identified as Alford Tynan."

Rubicoff paused to let this sink in. "Alford was an honor-
able man. He acknowledged his child and he provided for him."

At this point, Tolliver reclaimed his sneer. "So why isn't
his name Tynan if all this was done so honorably?"

"Who knows?" Rubicoff answered. "Probably because
Lillian wanted at least a show of respectability. She could pretend to be a widow if her last name and her son's last name
were the same."

Tallasee spoke up for the first time. "Why did you wait so
long to say anything?" she asked, speaking directly to me.

"You've known this all these years, but you still lived like that? We could have helped you."

I shrugged, while Rubicoff answered. "Sammy's reaction was much the same as Jenkins's. He waited because he didn't want to embarrass Mrs. Tynan. She always paid him well for his work and treated him kindly. He felt that it would be wrong to put her through it." I nodded my agreement. "As far as the way he lives, Sammy has grown accustomed to it. It hasn't been a hardship."

"Well, good," Tolliver said briskly, "because as far as I can see, nothing about his lifestyle will change. The old man's will was clear: I get control of the estate, and I can goddam well guarantee he ain't getting a dime." He stood to leave. "Thanks for sharing this sad story with us. Now tell your client to bugger off."

I chewed the inside of my cheek to keep from laughing. Tolliver was walking right into it.

"Hold on a moment, sir," Rubicoff said. "Perhaps you should take another look at your father's will. It does not leave control of the estate to you. It clearly says that in the event of his wife's death, control shall be passed to his eldest child."

He thumbed through some papers until he found one, which he held out to Tolliver. "Here's a copy of your own birth certificate. If you'll compare it to Sammy's, you'll see he was born six hours and thirty-three minutes before you.

"It's our contention that Sammy, being Alford's eldest child, now controls his estate."

Tolliver pulled a pair of reading glasses from his pocket and looked at his birth certificate, then picked up mine from the desk and looked at it. Under the stubble, his face was flushed. He set both papers down and looked at the administrator.

"They can't do this, can they? This is bullshit."

The administrator, obviously uncomfortable, met no one's eyes, instead speaking to a spot above Tolliver's shoulder. "Well, it all would be sorted out in court, of course. But it shouldn't be a big problem. Really, there's just the three of you involved. I'm sure some accommodation can be reached."

"Accommodation?" Tolliver said incredulously. "You mean you believe this fairy tale?"

"Mr. Tynan, be reasonable. Your father's will indeed says that his oldest living child shall take control of the estate. And from what I've seen here this morning, Mr. Rubicoff is prepared to make a very compelling case that Sammy is the oldest living child. It seems to me that the prudent course of action now is to talk to these two gentlemen."

From her seat, Tallasee spoke up. "He's right, Tolliver. For God's sake, stand next to him and look in the mirror. Across the eyes and nose, you're the same person."

Tolliver moved with a terrible burst of energy. He bounded across the office in two leaps and drove his shoulder under my chin just as I started to get up from my chair, nailing me into the wall with a linebacker's force. My head cracked back and hit so hard that the edges of my vision turned blurry. As I slid down the wall, I heard Tallasee screaming and saw Rubicoff and the administrator trying to pull Tolliver away. He shrugged them off and pounced on me, pushing me down to the floor and straddling me like a schoolyard bully, with his knees on my shoulder. With great roundhouse swings of his fists, he pounded the sides of my head, with each blow of that perverse cadence sending me deeper into the black that finally claimed me. The last thing I remember was his face, determined and emotionless.

◆ ◆ ◆

That queered my plan for him, of course. I'd known all along what I would do with Alford's money if I ever got it—which I did, despite Tolliver's effort to have the will voided. He filed the challenge himself, writing out the probate court lawsuit by hand in the prison library. But the judge dismissed it, pointedly noting in his order that Tolliver's standing in the matter would have been vastly better were he not serving a sentence for attempting to kill the heir apparent. So in due time, Alford's estate—grown to $23 million over the course of years—was passed to me.

I established two foundations. One of them is the Mountain Arts Foundation, which awards grants to help preserve the culture of the people of southern Appalachia, or something like that. Frankly, I don't know exactly what it does. Tallasee runs it with the $5 million I put up for it. But I'm sure you've seen those big, softcover books the foundation produces every year, each volume offering an exhaustive look at different country pursuits like quilt making and cabin building. They're bought by the thousands by affluent city folks who would be horrified if they ever had to actually take a midwinter dump in one of those culture-rich mountain outhouses.

The rest of the money went to Cot in the Closet, an organization that aids children who are left adrift in the world. It has facilities in twenty-three bus stations across the country, staffed around the clock by people trained to spot abandoned or runaway children. Rubicoff runs the whole enterprise, getting a fat, six-figure salary to actually do the work while I bask in the adoring limelight. I'd also planned on offering Tolliver a job with the organization, sweeping up around Cot in the Closet's Barrington facility, or perhaps tidying up the storeroom once occupied by the foundation's esteemed and revered founder. But his attempted-murder conviction killed that possibility. We can't have a violent felon around impressionable children, you know.

I thought about keeping some of the money for myself, but I couldn't make it taste right. I still get a queasy feeling when I see that picture of Perry Ray Pruitt dead on the church lawn. The money and the fire seem tied up together somehow. Perry Ray didn't want much more out of life than the chance to baptize a few sinners; but he never got it because I lost control over my own peculiar madness one night. So I gave all the money to the two foundations, except for what I needed to pay for a panel truck for the elder Mr. Pruitt. He's stocked it full of pamphlets, I hear, and has taken to preaching in parking lots while he stands on the bumper. Truth be told, Perry Ray just didn't have the old man's touch for it anyway.

So the only thing I actually got out of the inheritance was Maddie's house. She'd let things fall into disrepair as she got old, and it cost me thousands to fix the place up. By the time I was done, the money from my stock investments was almost all gone.

In fact, I used up the last bit of it to taunt Tolliver while he served his time. One day I hired a pair of strippers and a photographer from Atlanta to come to Barrington for a special assignment. I had my photograph taken with the women as we sat in Tolliver's childhood bed, me with an arm around each waist and a heavy naked breast hanging over each of my hands. I sent him an inscribed copy of the photo, along with a note saying that despite all our good times together, I'd managed to make new friends in his absence. You can't do too much for our boys in the penal system, you know.

The whole exercise cost a couple of thousand dollars, which was all I had left. I'd hoped Rubicoff might agree to call it a promotional expense and let Cot in the Closet pay for it, but he refused. So I'm broke. I'm back to doing chores again.

Sophie and I seem to spend a lot of time together. She comes from Atlanta on the bus almost every weekend, chattering away cheerfully from the time she gets here until her departure early Monday on that express run Burdeen finally managed to create. She's steadily undermining my theory that the total amount of happiness in a life can be measured in minutes, although she's balking at one thing: I can't get her to sneak into the bus station with me for a bit of slap-and-tickle on the old cot. She says the storeroom is haunted by the ghost of an old man who spent his life pretending to be deaf.

Funny thing, though. After Tolliver beat me that day in the lawyer's office, I began to notice that it became harder and harder to follow a conversation. People think I'm still pretending, but you know what? These days, I can't hear a thing.